THE CRYSTAL CAGE

THE CRYSTAL CAGE

by

Sandy Bayer

Boston ♦ Alyson Publications, Inc.

Typeset and printed in the United States of America.

This is a paperback original from Alyson Publications, Inc.,
40 Plympton St., Boston, Mass. 02118.
Distributed in England by GMP Publishers,
P.O. Box 247, London N17 9QR England.

This book is printed on acid-free, recycled paper.

First edition, first printing: September 1991

5 4 3 2 1

ISBN 1-55583-158-3

Dedicated to Rebecca

No one has given you any medals for your courage or determination or the way you keep smiling when others would have given up. All I have to give you is my love, and that I give you for a lifetime and beyond.

PROLOGUE

"Harold?"

"Hmm?"

"Larry thinks I'm going mad."

Dr. Harold Wolzinski stopped writing and peered over his glasses at the young woman sitting on the other side of the mahogany desk. Her voice had been so soft that he scarcely caught what she said.

He frowned and reached into the pocket of his white, crisply starched jacket, pulled out a handkerchief, and shook it out in a brisk snap. She jumped slightly.

"Sorry," he murmured.

She nodded. "I just seem to be so nervous these days."

He took off his glasses and began cleaning them, more to give himself time to think than because they really needed cleaning.

"You've always seemed pretty stable to me, Jeanne." He smiled. "What makes Larry think you're crazy?"

Jeanne Nowland gave a small, unconvincing shrug. Her hands, which had been clasped tightly in her lap, unclenched and fluttered a bit, and then were still again, the knuckles whitening as if she were making a valiant attempt to retain even a tenuous control over her emotions.

Wolzinski waited, but when nothing more was forthcoming, he said gently, "If you don't tell me what's wrong, I can't help you."

"Doctors always think they can help, don't they?"

Her faintly sarcastic tone startled him, and he glanced up from his glasses. Her eyes were closed. When she opened them, she looked toward the window to his right, avoiding his gaze.

"The baby," she said softly.

"I thought Stephanie was doing fine. Is there something you haven't told me?"

She shook her head slightly. "Not like what you mean." She stared down at her hands, and then, as though unable to bear his gaze any longer, she rose and walked to the window.

He watched as she moved, admiring the grace in her step, the fluid motion of thigh and hip beneath the light summer dress, the erect carriage of her body. As she reached the tall, arched window, the early-morning Boston sunlight played gently with her dark hair, caught back in what he thought was called a chignon, giving it almost blonde highlights. He felt a small catch in his chest, as though his heart had missed a beat and then thudded hard on the next one.

Glancing away, Wolzinski wondered for perhaps the thousandth time at the wisdom of his decision in taking his best friend's wife as his patient. He had fallen in love with her almost five years ago, from the first moment he had met her, he sometimes thought. But it had been too late even then, for she had already fallen in love with Lawrence Nowland. He finished cleaning his glasses, put his handkerchief back into his pocket, and closed the door to old, familiar feelings.

"What's wrong with the baby, Jeanne?"

She took a deep breath. "I don't know that there's anything wrong with her. You've been with her enough to know. She's a beautiful child. Bright, alert — loving." She smiled. "Larry says he can't wait for her first birthday. He wants to have a six-month birthday party for her on the twenty-seventh."

Wolzinski chuckled and put his glasses back on. He leaned back in the chair, swiveled it toward her, and lifted his feet to the corner of the desk. Clasping his hands behind his head, he said, "So why do you think you're going mad?" Before she could answer, he added, "Or is it really just Larry who's entertaining those thoughts?"

She gave him a small smile. "You always seem to know what I'm thinking, don't you?" Then she shook her head. "Things — happen. Things that just can't happen."

A twinge of a memory tugged at the edge of his mind, but he couldn't identify it, so he shook it off.

"Things like what?"

She folded her arms across her chest as if she were suddenly chilled. "I don't know. She just seems so — sensitive, I suppose the word is. Everything affects her. At the hospital, the head nurse on the floor would walk into the room, and Stephanie would suddenly start crying." She gestured vaguely. "She would be fine — gurgling away, almost smiling at me — and then this woman would walk in, and she'd start crying."

Wolzinski shrugged. "Coincidence. There's no other explanation that—"

Jeanne Nowland turned to face him. "*Every time*, Harold. *Every damned time.* The other nurses didn't have that effect on her. Nobody did." She paused, and when she spoke again, her voice had softened. "And it's still going on. Larry comes home and picks her up, and I can tell how he's feeling — what kind of day he's had — by looking at Stephanie. She's like a mirror of his emotions when he's holding her."

"And he hasn't noticed."

"I think he ignores it. He's afraid to see it."

Wolzinski frowned and looked down at the pencil he was holding as if he hadn't seen it before

"But that's not all of it." She rubbed her arms. "The other day, I was holding her on my lap, bouncing her, and she looked at me so — so strangely." She unfolded her arms, lifted her hand, and touched the window pane with her fingertips. "She just looked at me and touched my face. And then — it was as if she just — climbed into my head somehow." She frowned thoughtfully.

Wolzinski said nothing for a moment, then he cleared his throat. "I don't think I understand. She touched you, and then it seemed as if she climbed inside your head?" The memory was a twinge again, and he pushed it away more firmly in order to deal with the present.

Jeanne Nowland huffed in seeming exasperation and then muttered something under her breath.

"What?" Wolzinski queried.

She turned to face him fully. "I said, 'Men.' You and Larry were cut from the same cloth. Unless you can touch it or smell it or hear it or taste it or see it, you don't believe it exists. I didn't say she touched me and then—" She fluttered her hands in the air. "And then climbed inside my head. I said—" She stopped abruptly and turned away again. The silence in the brightly sunlit room grew for a few moments.

"Harold," she said softly, seeming to choose her words with care, "I know what I said. What I meant was that she entered my mind somehow. She didn't move her arms at all, and yet I felt her holding my face in her hands, patting my cheek." Jeanne lifted her hand and touched her face tentatively.

Wolzinski felt a tingle along the back of his neck. It was a strange sensation, as if the hair were rising, and it took him a moment to get past that sensation in order to respond.

"And Larry hasn't experienced anything like that?"

Jeanne lifted an eyebrow. It was an eloquent, though silent, reminder of what she had said already about men, he realized.

"And that's why Larry thinks you're going mad."

"He said there has to be a reasonable explanation for it. He said you could tell me what that reasonable explanation is." She folded her arms across her chest again, as if she already knew what his response would be and preferred to protect herself from it.

He looked down at his desk and shrugged before he brought his gaze back to hers. "I really don't know what to say. Sometimes new mothers feel depressed for a while after the baby is born. Maybe you're unconsciously mourning the closeness you felt with your child while she was in your womb. You're separate from her now, and maybe it was just that you wanted that again in some way." His own hands fluttered briefly as he unclasped them, and he stopped himself.

Jeanne stood and looked at him for long seconds from eyes that told him clearly that she did not believe his "reasonable explanation."

"Harold," she said, "I am telling you it happened." She looked back toward the window, and her voice grew even softer. "It *did* happen," she murmured, as if she finally had convinced herself. She returned her gaze to him, and when he said nothing, she shook her head in a gesture of resignation. Walking back to the chair, she lifted her purse from the corner of his desk. When she spoke again, her voice had become stronger, more assured.

"Larry wanted me to tell you. He thought I should because he thinks there's something wrong with me." She tucked her purse under her arm with an air of resolution. "There is nothing wrong with me. *Nothing.* If you're going to patronize me, I can go home and get that. And it won't cost me anything there. At least not any money."

She was at the door, her hand on the knob, before he could find his voice.

"Wait, Jeanne."

She turned back, looked at him, and saw something in his eyes she hadn't seen before. She took a step toward him. "You know something, don't you, Harold?"

"Look, Jeanne, I don't think that—"

"You know something you're not telling me. What is it?"

It was his turn to rise and walk to the window. The huge trees overlooking the square a block from his office were majestic. It had rained the night before, and they looked darker, fuller. After a moment, he allowed his memory to be tugged back to

February. To a bleak, icy snowstorm that had taken even Boston by surprise.

The memory lay in a dimly lit hospital corridor in the predawn hours of a particularly black night. He had been leaving the nursery when the young, blonde nurse had stopped him in the hall. He frowned. What was her name? Baker? No, longer. Brubaker. His frown of concentration increased.

Suddenly, the nurse's voice seemed to break into his consciousness.

"The Nowland baby. She touched me, Doctor. Like she was — was inside my mind. Only she was just lying there, with her eyes closed. But I felt it. As if she were touching me. Patting my face."

He suggested to the nurse that she take some time off — maybe transfer off the graveyard shift. There were some people who simply couldn't deal with the changes required for working while the rest of the world slept. He watched as her face reflected a certain resignation, as if she had been told that too many times already.

A couple of weeks later, he asked the nurse's supervisor and found that she was still working the same shift with apparently no problems. He dismissed the incident as having occurred from overwork, perhaps too little sleep. He had not made a connection between her apparent adjustment to the work schedule and the fact that the Nowland baby was no longer in the hospital nursery.

"What do you know, Harold?"

Jeanne Nowland's voice broke through the fog of memory, more strident this time, startling him.

"I'm sorry. I was remembering something a nurse said to me while you and Stephanie were still in the hospital." He turned and watched her face change as he told her of the incident. Afterwards, there was relief written there; her features relaxed, and she closed her eyes briefly as he finished. When she opened them, though, the relief had turned to fear.

"My God, Harold," she said softly, "what is it? Could it be some sort of — hallucination or something?" She shook her head. "No. I know it happened. And there were two different times and two different people who felt it." She placed her fingertips to her lips, and he saw a tear pool at the corner of her eye.

He looked down at his desk and then removed his glasses again, took out the handkerchief, and began cleaning them, not looking at her.

"It may be more than two people. I just—" He cleared his throat. "I just remembered something else." He shook his head slightly. "Really, Jeanne, I had forgotten all of this. I chalked it up to other things. A person's mind plays tricks sometimes, you know." He put his glasses on, but he still did not look at her fully.

"Remember when I came over for dinner a couple of weeks ago and you and I went up to see Stephanie before I left?" Out of the corner of his eye, he saw her nod. "When we left the nursery, you went first. I was going to close the door so the light in the hall wouldn't keep her awake. When I turned around, the light was falling across her face, and her eyes were open. She was looking at me. It was such a — a sweet look, I couldn't keep myself from smiling at her."

He looked up to see Jeanne staring intently at him. "As I started to close the door, you put your hand on mine." He cleared his throat and looked away again, willing himself to say what he had to say in order to give her the peace of knowing her sanity, at least, was intact. "It was a very light touch — almost a caress. As if it were just your fingertips." He cleared his throat once more and put on his glasses.

"But I don't remember—"

"I know. When I turned to look at you, you were all the way down the hall, at the top of the stairs. There was no way you could have touched me when I thought you had."

He leaned back in the chair. Picking up a pencil, he turned it end over end for several seconds.

"It startled me. I had felt your hand just an instant before, and there you were down a long hallway. Much too far away." He shrugged. "Sometimes your mind plays tricks on you, I thought. I assumed you had touched my hand but that it had taken a moment to register because I was so absorbed in looking at the baby. You know," he said, glancing at her now, "it was a little like when you're driving and your mind's somewhere else, and you look up and find you've gone twenty miles and don't know how you got there." His voice trailed off. "A little like that, maybe."

He removed his glasses and rubbed the bridge of his nose. "Please understand. I didn't say anything because I didn't know it was something I should have told you." He put his glasses back on. She was staring at him.

"Are you saying it was Stephanie who touched you? Across the room?" She paused, waiting for his answer. "Harold?"

He said nothing, because there was nothing he could think to say. Absolutely nothing.

Harold Wolzinski possessed a mind with a scientific bent that he had honed over the years in medical school and in his private practice. It was a mind that rebelled now at accepting the impossibility of what was being allowed entrance. As he sat there, silent, it slid out file drawers of manila folders jammed with evidence, piled the folders on the desk in front of him. It pulled medical journals from their binders on his bookshelves, rifled through their pages, and lifted them for his inspection to prove to him that what he was thinking was impossible.

Jeanne Nowland was staring at him, not seeing him, looking through him.

A chill crossed the back of his neck again. If it was so impossible, then why had it seemed so real?

Both of the women had said it.

The baby touched me.

His mind's rebellion notwithstanding, another part of himself — he wondered if it might not be his soul — knew it was true.

Because the baby had touched him, too.

He turned the pencil end over end, while the silence in the room seemed to deepen.

PART
ONE

FRIDAY

19

DECEMBER

1980

1

"Karen. This woman doesn't want to meet me. I don't want to meet her. Why are you doing this?"

Stephanie Nowland sat on the side of the king-size bed, held the telephone receiver between her ear and one hunched shoulder, and fumbled to get a cigarette out of a freshly opened pack. Placing the cigarette between her lips, she tossed the pack onto the nightstand and reached for the lighter. She squinted her eyes against the smoke that curled up and lay back on the bed. "You're going to keep at me until I say 'yes,' aren't you?" She smiled slightly as she heard Dr. Karen Fowler chuckle at the other end of the line.

"Stephanie, all I'm asking you to do is meet her. I can't for the life of me figure out why the two of you have such a problem with this. She keeps telling me that she has no time. Okay, well, I know she's working on her doctorate, and I know she's got teaching duties this semester, but enough is enough.

One simple little party is all I'm asking from either of you. Just one simple little party. And at least she's got an excuse. Several of them, actually. I still haven't heard even one of yours."

Stephanie rubbed at her eyes with the back of her hand. "I told you, I've got a lot of clients right now. I'm booked solid."

"Right. You've got seventeen people coming over for psychic readings tonight." Karen harrumphed in mild exasperation. "Stephanie?"

"Mmm."

"You remember when your car broke down that time you were halfway to Jax and I came and picked you up?"

Stephanie shook her head and grinned. "Of course."

"Well," Karen said, "I'm calling in the favor."

Stephanie tried to suppress a laugh and failed. "That's blackmail."

"That's the way the world runs. Or so I learned from my Puerto Rican grandmother. By the way, have I ever told you how psychic she was?"

"You have." Stephanie found it hard to stop smiling.

"Well, I inherited some of it. And I'm telling you, it's time for you to meet Marian. Tonight."

"I thought she wasn't coming to the party."

Karen chuckled. "Let's just say I've got another favor to call in. The only thing you have to do is say you'll come."

"Have you done any other favors for me that I'm going to hear about later?"

"Not a one. This will clear the slate."

"Why do I distrust that?"

"Because you're a naturally distrusting person?"

Stephanie laughed again, but there was a short silence, and then Karen said softly, "Stephanie?"

"Mmm."

"You know it's time to meet her, don't you? I can feel it."

Stephanie stubbed out the cigarette in the ashtray on the nightstand and rubbed her eyes. "Karen," she said, "I've had a lot of painful relationships. I'm not sure I'm ready for another one right now." She felt, rather than heard, a certain intensity in Karen's voice.

"Not this time. Not this time, my friend."

"Is that a guarantee?"

"As much a guarantee as you'll get in this life, dear," Karen responded.

A few minutes later, the conversation over, Stephanie placed the telephone receiver back in its cradle and went to stand in front of the dresser mirror. Sighing heavily, she brushed her fingers through her hair, then stepped back and tried to see herself as someone else might see her.

Before her was the reflection of a woman in her midthirties, slightly on the lean side, with short, dark hair lightly streaked with silver. Down the left side of her face lay the scar. She touched it, felt the familiar heavy weight in the middle of her chest, and, with a practiced mental hand, brushed it away. Combing her fingers through her hair again, she wished that she had gotten it trimmed the day before. She briefly considered calling Sidney to see if she could get a haircut. Then, in slight disbelief, she shook her head.

"This is insane," she muttered at her image. "I haven't even met this woman."

"This woman" was a friend whom Karen had been trying for several months to convince Stephanie to meet. The occasion that evening was the seasonal party for friends and the teaching staff at the liberal arts college where Karen's husband, Bob, taught a graduate seminar in psychology. One of his teaching assistants was Marian Damiano — "this woman." According to Karen, she and Bob occasionally got together with Marian for dinner and an evening of incredibly stimulating talk, mostly because Marian was "such a fascinating person." It was but one of the many sterling qualities that Karen had reported so glowingly in an attempt to persuade Stephanie's cooperation in the matchmaking attempt.

Stephanie smiled at her reflection. Karen possessed a seemingly fragile femininity that masked an iron core of pure will. And when she had set her mind on something, she was anything but subtle. If Stephanie had believed everything Karen had told her, she would be preparing right now to meet a person who was a combination of Meryl Streep, Barbara Walters, and Mother Teresa.

Stephanie's connection was also with Bob, who had consulted her, although somewhat reluctantly he later admitted, about a client he had been seeing in his private practice. The client had been obsessed with the idea that when she went to sleep, she was going to be confronted by an evil spirit and would never wake up. Following Stephanie's assistance with his client, she and Bob had become friends, and she had eventually met Karen.

Stephanie frowned slightly and leaned closer to the mirror. The silver over her temples was more noticeable with each passing year. Although her hair was much darker than her mother's, it had always had the same fine texture and softness. Now, the silver was appearing the same way her mother's had in her midthirties. But her mother's influence on her looks had softened her father's contribution of a jawline that made her face appear stern at times.

And in terms of her personality, she considered, her parents had passed on traits that seemed to parallel her physical features. Her father, who had died from a heart attack when Stephanie was twelve, had been a man of unbending principles who expected nothing but the best effort from himself and those around him. They were admirable traits for a corporate attorney, but in a father, they sometimes prevented the closeness his two daughters had wanted. Her mother, on the other hand, had supplied the gentleness, the touching. It had protected Stephanie and guided her through the pain of those early years as she came to terms with what some had seen as a gift and others had seen as a mark of some hidden, perhaps evil, force.

She stepped back and tried smiling at her reflection, but her anxiety made the smile appear sick. She'd read once that Queen Elizabeth's face was so stern-looking that she had trained herself to smile almost constantly in public. If she didn't, the press would almost invariably report the next day that "the Queen appeared displeased." Stephanie groaned. She had enough problems herself without dwelling on those of the Queen of England. She glanced at the clock on the nightstand. The morning was getting old, and for some strange reason, she felt as if she had a million things to do.

Regardless of that feeling, though, she did little else the rest of the day but wander from room to room in the small, two-bedroom house she had bought two years before, straightening up what was, in truth, very little clutter. It was only when she entered the bedroom again and began changing the bed linens that she realized with a start what she had been doing. She was standing by the bed, holding a pillow under her chin to slip a pillowcase onto it, when the realization struck her. And it struck her so hard that she dropped the pillow onto the bed and sat down heavily.

She was preparing for this woman she had not yet met as if the woman were to be her lover. She frowned. No. More. As if this woman had been her lover for many years, had been on a long trip, and was now coming home.

She probed her memory of the afternoon and realized that this was not the only preposterous idea she had entertained during her wanderings around the house, although the other was similar to the first. She used this room as her bedroom, and the other bedroom, a larger one at the front of the house, she kept as an office where she met with clients. As she sifted through her memory, she discovered that she had been musing on whether her office could be divided by another wall and thereby used by two people. As she cleaned, she had been wondering whether the house might be too small for two people.

She sat on the bed for long minutes, carefully considering what her thoughts might mean, unwilling to simply accept them at face value, unwilling yet to give credence to Karen's words.

She was not ready, she argued with herself this time, for another painful relationship. There had been more than she cared to think about, and all of them had been short-lived, she felt, because of the wall that seemed to remain in place even when she was with those she deeply cared about. For the last two years, she had been alone by choice, and if they had been years that held loneliness from time to time, they also had been years of relative inner peace. She was not sure that she cared to have that peace disturbed. She was not at all sure — regardless of the thoughts she apparently had been entertaining just below her consciousness.

The next few hours were spent in trying to keep her mind off the party — an event that she told herself she would not have attended had she not promised Karen. But as the day wore on toward evening, a growing feeling of anticipation asserted itself against all she did to push it aside. She found herself looking through her closet for a pair of gray dress slacks that she had not worn for some time. She tried on and discarded three shirts before she found the one she ultimately chose to wear. As she put on the last shirt, a white, tailored one open deeply at the throat, she caught a glimpse of herself again in the dresser mirror across the room.

In that split instance, there was a flash of chestnut hair falling across her vision, the murmur of a sweetly familiar laugh she knew she had never heard before, the achingly sensual fragrance of a body she had never known, the silkiness of heated skin beneath her hands — startling, sea green eyes that seemed to penetrate to the bottom of her soul. They filled her senses in a rush that left her knees weak. And she knew clearly in that brief moment, as she stared into her own dark eyes so far away, that there would never be anything more right in her life than what was waiting for her now.

2

When Stephanie arrived, the party was in full swing. Making her way through the throng of people, she found her senses assaulted by the mental undercurrents surrounding her. Normally, the crystal-fine psychic curtain she pulled around herself kept her from being overwhelmed by the thoughts and feelings of others. How much filtered through depended a great deal on the strength of others' thoughts and emotions, and what she had found over the years was that while alcohol, at some point, might relax inhibitions about behavior, it also seemed to strengthen those thoughts and emotions. The crowded room pressed in on her. She pulled the curtain more tightly around herself and made her way toward the kitchen.

Karen, a petite woman whose frame contained an energy that appeared to Stephanie as a vibrating, coiled spring at times, held a broom in her hand and was reaching for a dustpan when Stephanie found her. Broken glass lay on the floor. When she saw Stephanie, she pointed to the glass.

"Next year, I'm getting this thing catered, I don't care how much it costs. And I sure as hell don't care what Bob says about it." Stephanie moved to help and was waved aside.

Sweeping up the glass efficiently and then setting the broom aside, Karen flashed a sudden smile. "Marian's in the library. I'll introduce you." She started across the room, but Stephanie's outstretched hand stopped her.

"That's okay. I know where the library is."

Karen studied her for a moment, obviously puzzled, then she shrugged. But as Stephanie turned to leave, Karen said quietly, "You know, that feeling about the two of you — I feel a little silly about it, but—"

Stephanie shook her head. "Don't feel silly." She paused. "You know, after we talked this morning, it occurred to me that perhaps you're even more psychic than you think." As she reached the door, she turned back. "By the way, I'd like to meet your grandmother some time." She smiled and left Karen with both eyebrows raised in inquiry.

As Stephanie stood in front of the closed library door, she hesitated as she touched the doorknob. A wave of warmth seemed to radiate from the door and press against her skin, and she allowed it to penetrate her senses. It was an incredibly sensual feeling, and she closed her eyes to savor its full effect. The words *coming home* drifted through her mind. After a moment, she opened her eyes again, and then she opened the door, stepped inside, and closed it behind her.

A woman stood in her stockinged feet in front of the built-in bookshelves across the room, bent slightly to study the titles on the bottom shelf. A softly flowing dress hugged her breasts, clung to her waist, and fell in provocative folds over her hips. Wavy, chestnut hair cascaded down the side of her face, and she pushed it back as she straightened. The sea green eyes met Stephanie's across the room.

Stephanie felt her body respond in that first instant with an intensity that she had not believed possible. Her breath caught in her throat as the essence of the woman — Marian — engulfed her, flowed around her. The curtain she protected herself behind fell gently away, and she scarcely noticed its absence. Taking a deep breath and releasing it slowly, she watched as Marian took in the physical details as she had.

In an almost involuntary reaction, she shoved her hands into the pockets of her slacks. She stood under the gaze of those eyes and felt herself falling into the warmth and vulnerability she had sensed before she entered the room. She wanted to gather the woman into her arms and touch the silky hair, look deeply into the eyes that were edged with fine laugh lines and held so much tenderness and wisdom and strength. Her palms sensed the heated curves under the dress, the warmth of the breasts, the full hips.

Then the sensing was no longer enough. She wanted to touch Marian fully, make love to her — become one with her. And the instant the thought entered her consciousness, she knew it was a dangerous one. No sooner had she entertained it than she felt herself being drawn into Marian's mind.

She saw the puzzled look and tried to withdraw. It was late, though, too late, and she found it hard to retreat. But then, as she struggled, she realized with surprise that there was consent, a willingness that she didn't understand. All she knew was that it was there — and that it felt right. And so she surrounded Marian with as much gentleness as she could and stepped fully inside her mind.

It was not a new sensation for Stephanie. Since as far back as she could remember, she had been able to enter others' consciousness almost at will. Doing so seemed to be simply a matter of letting the protective psychic curtain drift away and then projecting herself past her own physical body. It took little effort to accomplish, and, in fact, there were times, such as now, when the pull from outside herself seemed so great that it would have taken a great deal of effort to prevent it.

Time slowed, quickened, finally lost all meaning. She felt herself smiling, drifting into a warmth that pulled at her heart. She was walking through hallways in what seemed to be a huge, old Victorian house. Doorways opened to either side as she passed, revealing rooms filled with Marian's past — the laughter and tears, the loving, the excitement, and the struggles of a lifetime. It was a warm house, where feelings were allowed to flow with freedom, not bottled up in dingy corners to build into small hates and fears. As she reached a staircase that curved to an upper floor, she smiled. There was a soft voice calling to her.

She climbed the stairs and made her way down a hallway that was glassed in on one side by windows that overlooked a forest dappled by sunlight. At the end of the hallway was a door that opened as she reached it, revealing a bedroom filled with magnificent tropical plants, heady fragrances of flowers, and the slow circling of a fan overhead.

In the middle of the room was a huge, canopied bed draped with dark green and pastel-printed sheets. Marian waited for her there, her naked body gleaming in the glow of a candle that stood on a table beside the bed. Her eyes smiled at Stephanie, and she lifted a hand in a welcoming gesture.

Then Stephanie, naked herself, was enfolding Marian in her arms, tasting her mouth, feeling Marian's hands on her shoulders, and she was making long, slow love to her, being gentle and then sweetly rough at times, luxuriating in the warmth and silkiness of Marian's body, inhaling Marian's fragrance, hearing the little gasps and breaths against her face, anticipating the small cries and opening her mouth against Marian's mouth, and as she caught the cries and the soft, low moans in her own throat, she took Marian toward a joining, a merging of senses that had been unknown to her before.

Afterwards, after what seemed to be both an eternity and the flash of an instant, as carefully as she could, with the same gentleness she had entered, she withdrew.

A moment later, she found herself, shaken, completely within her own body again. She stood there, orienting herself, watching as Marian, lips parted and eyes slightly unfocused, came back to herself as well. Stephanie smiled gently, apologetically, and moved forward, taking her hands out of her pockets and outstretching one.

"Ms. Damiano, I presume," she murmured, taking Marian's hand in her own.

Marian leaned against the railing of the fishing pier that extended from the rear of the Lighthouse restaurant and looked eastward toward a slight rise, where the black-and-white striped lighthouse that gave the restaurant its name stabbed through the tangle of live oaks into the early-morning sky. She brushed her hair back against the chill wind that had picked up since they left the restaurant and pulled her windbreaker more closely around her. Turning her gaze toward Stephanie, she spoke, her voice gentle.

"You said last night—" She smiled slightly. "Well, I suppose it was early this morning — that you'd tell me 'sometime soon' about the scar. Did you mean soon like today — or like in a few years?"

Stephanie returned the smile. "Does that mean you intend to be around for at least a few years?"

Marian chuckled. "I could say you're reading too much into that, but it would sound unbearably coy, and I don't feel like being coy. If I don't answer your question, does that mean you won't answer mine?"

"No." Stephanie looked toward the lighthouse, the smile gone."Do you really want to know?"

"I learned a long time ago not to ask questions I didn't want to hear the answers to. But it's obviously an issue that you find hard to deal with. I'm not going to press you."

Stephanie was silent for a moment, and when she finally spoke, the words seemed to be wooden blocks she was placing on a table in front of her. "I have a sister — Caroline — who's a year older. When I was young, I found it very hard to control — my mind, the psychic energy, whatever you want to call it. One day, when I was about six, Caroline and I were playing, and we got into an argument." She frowned, as if she were studying the blocks, trying to understand what her words meant. "She was getting angrier and angrier, and I felt as if I were drowning in her anger." She shook her head slightly. "I didn't have those words then, of course. I only remember the pain and confusion I was feeling." She took a deep breath and let it out slowly, and the blocks seem to melt away until there was only pain left behind.

"It was like a tidal wave. I felt as if I were smothering. I tried to close it out. My mother had told me to try thinking about a curtain surrounding me, keeping out others' thoughts. But it was a case of too little and much too late. It was as if Caroline were inside my head, filling it with so much anger that I couldn't think my own thoughts." She turned to look at Marian. "Am I making any sense? Am I saying this so you can understand any of it?"

"I can't understand completely, of course," Marian said softly, "but I used to get into arguments with my ex-husband. I felt overwhelmed by his anger at times. There seemed to be something irrational about it. He'd get so angry about even little things that he would seem — out of control, I suppose. And I'd be terribly confused by his anger and his yelling. It was as if he were hammering at me mentally. I couldn't even think. All I felt like doing was curling up in a ball to protect myself."

Her brows knitted together. "I guess that's as close as I can come to understanding what you're describing."

"It's close enough." Stephanie rubbed at her eyes and sighed. "Just as I thought I had succeeded in closing myself off, I saw a knife in Caroline's hand." She shook her head. "At first, I wasn't sure it was real. I don't know where she got it. It was a little penknife. Maybe she found it somewhere. All I know is that she came at me with the knife, and I put my hands up to ward her off. Or at least that's what I thought I was doing. Maybe I didn't even move them.

"I pushed at her. Whether it was just mentally or whether I pushed her physically, too, I don't know. I was scared. The next minute, my mother was standing there, and Caroline was on the ground, her eyes rolled back in her head. She was in the middle of a grand mal seizure. I didn't know then what was wrong with her, of course." Stephanie looked toward the water. "After she spent several days in the hospital, she was taken to a mental institution. She's been there ever since."

Marian put her hand out and touched Stephanie's arm. "Stef, you were six years old. You were scared. Whatever happened to your sister, you were just protecting yourself."

"She's spent the last twenty-nine years in a mental institution because of me."

"Have you seen her?"

Stephanie uttered a short, bitter laugh. "Oh, yes, I've seen her. A few weeks after it happened, my mother took me. I walked into the room, and she screamed in terror and ran to crouch in a corner. My mother didn't take me any more. When I got older, I went to see her on my own. The same thing happened. By looking at me, of course, there was no way she could have known it was me. Not that many years later. But she knew. She still knew." Her voice grew softer. "After it happened three or four times, I stopped going."

Marian put her arm around Stephanie's waist. "I'm sorry," she whispered. "But I really can't believe it's your fault." She frowned slightly. "Did your sister have the same kind of — mental power that you do?"

Stephanie shook her head. "I don't know. I seem to remember something like that when we were kids, but I can't really remember. And my mother seemed to think she didn't. But how else would she have known it was me?"

"Maybe she had the potential for it, but it got twisted around for her."

Stephanie sighed again. "I don't know."

They stood silent for several moments, watching as the wind rippled the surface of the water.

"You know," Stephanie said, "I haven't told many people that whole story before. Just a few close friends, really. I usually don't mention that I have a sister. It seems easier not to."

Marian smiled gently and took Stephanie's hand. "Well, I feel quite honored that you felt you could tell me."

"Well, my feeling was that I was going to have to tell you sooner or later."

Marian glanced at her, one eyebrow uplifted. "Are you saying you think I have the capacity to be a nag?"

Stephanie grinned. "I would never say that."

Marian laughed in response. "I think you know me too well already." She studied Stephanie for a moment. "You know, I had this whole thing made up in my mind that the scar had something to do with your work with the police. Finding murderers and all. Maybe one got too close."

Stephanie gave her a wry smile. "I'm usually not so much in the thick of things as to be in danger. Most of it has to do with finding missing persons. Those who want to be found, anyway." She paused. "There have been very few killers thus far."

"Thus far?"

"Mmm. Two." A frown flitted across Stephanie's face. "Both times, I had nightmares about them. Once I contacted the police, the nightmares stopped." She ran her fingers through her hair. "The police followed a couple of leads and wrapped up everything."

"They must have been some pretty strong leads."

Stephanie shrugged slightly. "I suppose. Eventually, they would've done it anyway, though."

Marian studied Stephanie for a moment and then smiled. "Why do I have the feeling that there was a lot more to your part than that?"

Stephanie shrugged again.

"You said 'thus far,'" Marian said. "That sounds like you believe there'll be more."

"Somewhere down the road. Maybe a couple of years. No longer than that." A frown flitted across her face, and her voice was quiet. "Sometimes I feel really scared."

Marian reached out and took Stephanie's hand. They spent the next few moments looking out across the water, watching the gulls circling the lighthouse, and it was Marian who broke the silence this time, her voice soft, almost hesitant.

"You know, I've never made love like that before. I've always held something back. I wasn't holding anything back last night." A faint blush appeared on her cheeks that was not caused by the warmth of the early-morning sun.

"I know."

Marian chuckled and leaned sideways against the railing so she could look at Stephanie's face. "Yes, I suppose you do." She lifted her hand and brushed the backs of her fingers against Stephanie's cheek. "I wonder if that could be a problem at times."

"I'm not privy to all your thoughts, you know. In fact, most of the time, I manage to keep a reasonable psychic distance between myself and others." Stephanie looked out at the shallow, grassy water near the shoreline so she was facing away from Marian. When she looked back, her expression was one of concern. "Actually, the emotional distance may be more of a problem for you. When I'm around other people, I tend to keep that — curtain, I suppose you could call it — between myself and others so that I don't intrude on them. And so they don't intrude on me. Intimacy is sometimes a problem because of that. I knew the moment I opened myself to you last night that a real priority for you is emotional closeness." She paused. "Marian — I've become used to not having it. I don't think you could live without it."

Another long silence ensued while Marian studied Stephanie carefully, then she glanced away. "I think it's strange that you say that. I've never experienced any closer emotional intimacy with anyone in my life than I did last night. Not when I was with you — not even before, when you walked into that room, and I—"

"Marian. I never meant for that to happen. I didn't know it was going to happen. It just—"

Marian closed her eyes briefly and shook her head. "No. Let me finish." She opened her eyes and looked intently into Stephanie's for a moment, and then she looked away again. Her voice was ragged. "I can't look at you while I say this." She took a deep breath and exhaled before she spoke again.

"When you came into that room, you didn't just walk into my head. You walked into my heart, too. Maybe into my soul. And you know that. I felt as if we were one person. I couldn't tell where I stopped and you began. When you left — when you walked out of my head again — I felt more alone than I've ever felt in my life. But I also never felt closer to another human being than I did right then. As if, for the first time, someone knew me inside and out. All my faults and insecurities. And all my strengths and — wonderfulness. No having to find the right words. No explanations necessary."

Stephanie shook her head slightly, and there was pain in her eyes when Marian looked at her again.

"You don't know what you'd be getting into. Most of the time—"

Marian lifted her hand and put a gentle finger against Stephanie's lips. "Shh. Let me finish. I know that everything I'm going to say, you already know. But I need to say it. To make it real so I don't try to hide it from myself." She waited for Stephanie's nod before she continued.

"When I went back to my apartment last night, after the party, I couldn't sleep. I couldn't get my mind off you. I wanted you more than I've ever wanted anyone in my life. When I finally called you at two-thirty, it was because I couldn't stand being away from you another minute. I couldn't stand not having your hands on me. I felt as if my whole body ached from wanting you." She looked into Stephanie's eyes, and her voice became almost a whisper.

"And I was willing to trust more of myself with you than I ever have with anyone. For a long time, I've wanted someone who would take me to bed and make love to me as if I belonged to her. That was why I didn't want you to come to my place. I wanted to be in your bed. I wanted you to be in control. Totally. That was important to me." A faint blush covered her cheeks again, and she looked down briefly and chuckled. "A pretty old-fashioned, romantic notion. It's also more than a little politically incorrect, I'm afraid."

Stephanie grinned. "I'm not sure I believe you run your life according to what you think might be politically correct."

Marian laughed softly. "Well, my friend, I used to make an attempt once in a while." She lifted an eyebrow and looked at Stephanie. "I feel as if you're trying to sidetrack me. Are you embarrassed by what I'm saying?"

Stephanie smiled. "A little." She looked away and then caught Marian's eyes again. "But only from pleasure, I assure you. I'm used to dealing with other people's emotions almost constantly, but it's usually on a wordless basis. Hearing them expressed out loud seems to require a response. And expressing my own emotions is very difficult most of the time."

"I need words sometimes," Marian said gently.

"I know." Stephanie stared at the ripple of waves as another gust of wind blew across the water. "Yesterday afternoon, after I talked to Karen and agreed to meet you, I got a strong — impression of what was coming. Of you. I had the idea that—" She shook her head. "I'm sorry. I'm afraid if I say it—" She looked at Marian. "It's too soon. Too frightening because it feels too right."

Marian squeezed Stephanie's hand. "Say it," she whispered. "I can't say it all, Stef. It *is* too frightening. I don't understand it."

Stephanie looked out at the water again. "I felt as if you were — coming home to me. As if you had been gone a very long time, and you were coming home." Her voice almost broke. "I felt as if you and I had been together a lifetime and had somehow been separated. It was if I had been looking for you and had finally found you again."

There was a long silence, and then Marian whispered, "Coming home. Yes. That's what it was like."

For minutes, both of them stared out across the water and watched as the wind whipped the grasses at the edge of the marshy land. Finally, Marian released Stephanie's hand, reached into the pocket of her jeans, and brought out a Kleenex to wipe at her eyes. When she looked back at Stephanie, Stephanie had turned toward her, a question in her eyes that was almost a plea.

Marian smiled and lifted a hand to touch Stephanie's cheek again. "Don't worry. I'm not going to get scared off. I'm frightened by how fast this is happening, but that's my head talking. It tends to be a good deal more practical than my heart. And I'm willing to let my heart have its way this time." She paused. "Actually, I'm not sure my head even has a chance."

"Oh," Stephanie said with a wry smile, "if you wanted your head to have a chance, I think it would."

Marian chuckled. "I suppose you're right." A twinkle appeared in her eyes. "You know, the truth is that at this particular moment, my head and heart seem to be receding into the background."

"They are?"

Marian took Stephanie's hand in hers and looked down at it. Her voice was soft, throaty. "Right now, I want your hands on me again. I want you to undress me. Very slowly and with a great deal of care." She looked into Stephanie's eyes. "I undressed for you last night. I saw how you watched me, how you wanted me. When I finished, I felt more naked, more vulnerable than I ever have in my life. And I felt more protected and taken care of than ever before. I want to feel that again. I want to be in your bed, your hands on me, your mouth on me. I want to feel you next to me, holding me, inside of me. I want you to be gentle with me, rough with me, whatever you want." Her voice trembled. "I'm crazy with wanting you right now, Stef."

Stephanie swallowed hard, and her voice was a rasp when she spoke. "I've never wanted anyone the way I want you."

A slow smile spread across Marian's face. "Well, dear, for not being very good with expressing yourself in words, I'd say you've just done quite well." She grabbed Stephanie's hand and began pulling her along the pier back toward the restaurant.

Laughing, Stephanie resisted. "Can I assume we're going to my house?"

Marian turned and lifted an eyebrow. "Why, I thought you knew." She put her arms around Stephanie and held her close for a moment, her voice serious now. "I'm not sure yet. It's going to take a while for both of us to be sure. But I think we're going home." She pulled back slightly to look at Stephanie. "I really think maybe we're going home."

"Helen! Where's my damn glove, honey?"

Helen Jacobson paused the applesauce-laden spoon half-way to her year-old daughter's opening mouth and turned her head toward her lover's voice. "In the hall closet," she called. "Behind the tent." She shook her head and turned back to Katie, who had decided to finger-paint her highchair tray with applesauce.

A moment later, Beatrice Woodward's short, muscular frame appeared in the doorway. Woody wiggled her hand into the outfielder's glove and smacked a fist into it. "I gotta get some leather soap. I should've used it before I put the glove away."

Helen wiped Katie's face with a damp paper towel, and the little girl uttered a shrieking laugh as Woody waved the glove at her. Picking up the spoon in a pudgy fist, she banged it on the tray.

"Woody," Helen said, "don't you get her started again. She needs a nap, and if you get her worked up, she'll take just that much longer to get to sleep. I've got things to do."

Woody grinned, waved the glove again, and was rewarded with another shriek.

"Woody!"

"Ahh, say, 'Don't sweat it, Momma. Woody's gonna take care of me.'" She put the glove down and pulled Katie out of the highchair. "Ain't that right, Katie?"

Helen shook her head, a smile starting. "You going to give her a bath later?"

"Yep." Woody leaned down and kissed the corner of Helen's mouth. "Look," she said gently, "you look tired. Why don't you lie down for a while? Katie and I'll be just fine. Okay?"

Helen, a bit leaner and taller than her partner, stood and draped her arm over Woody's free shoulder. "Are you sure? Maybe I should put her down for her nap first."

"Go," Woody said sternly. With one hand, she turned Helen and gave her a gentle push toward the door. "Remember Jan and Ellen are coming over for cards tonight. I don't want to have to explain why your head fell in the chip dip. They'll think I'm not taking care of my woman."

Helen chuckled. "I suppose I could use a little rest."

"That's right." Woody nodded her head in agreement. "And Katie and I will go out and play a fast game of catch, and we'll be right in, ain't that right, Kates?" She bounced the little girl on her shoulder and laughed when Katie screamed with glee and grabbed at her hair.

Helen shook her head, still smiling, and left the room.

Half an hour later, Woody watched as Katie finally fell asleep, then she leaned over the railing of the crib and smoothed back the fine blonde hair from the child's forehead. "Katie," she whispered, "you and me are going to make great pals, you know that? And it doesn't matter what you decide you want to do with your life, either. You want to be a lawyer, that's great. You want to drive trucks or be a dancer or a waitress or a teacher — just as long as you're happy, Katie.

That's all I want for you. If you like girls, we can talk about that, and if you like boys, we can talk about that, too."

She smiled and straightened. "I gotta tell you, though, Kates, I don't know much about boys. I guess we'll just have to play it by ear if you go that route." She released a contented sigh. "But remember this, no matter what you want, I'll be here for you. Okay? I'll always be here." After another minute, she left and gently closed the door behind her.

Helen mumbled sleepily as Woody lay down beside her on the bed. Turning, she put an arm over Woody's waist and snuggled close. She mumbled again.

Woody chuckled softly. "What was that?"

"Mmm. I said, 'Is Katie asleep?'"

"Yep," Woody whispered. "Now go back to sleep. I didn't mean to wake you up."

"I wasn't asleep. I've just been resting my eyes."

"Right."

"No, really."

Woody smiled and put her arm under Helen's head and pulled her closer. "Well, try and sleep now."

"Mmm." Helen sighed and snuggled her face against Woody's shoulder. "I'm glad you're here."

Woody kissed the dark blonde hair that fell across Helen's forehead. "Me, too," she whispered. "Now sleep."

Seconds later, Helen's breathing changed subtly as she drifted into what was apparently a deep sleep. But Woody found that, although she was tired from what had been a long week, she could not join Helen. Something her partner had said the night before at dinner kept playing in her mind, keeping her awake.

Doug says he's going to fight for Katie.

Helen had just sat down at the table when she said it. The statement seemed unusually loud, and it took Woody a couple of seconds to process the meaning.

"What?"

Helen avoided Woody's eyes. "Doug called me at work this afternoon and said he's thinking about getting in touch with his lawyer. He says—" Her voice almost broke. She took a deep breath, released it, and began again. "He says a friend of his told him I was living with a dyke, and that he doesn't want his daughter being brought up by queers." When she finally turned her eyes toward Woody, they were filled with tears. "I'm scared," she whispered. "I'm really scared."

Woody sat there, helpless to move for several seconds, her stomach sinking into an ice-water bath of fear. But a moment later, the anger took over, and she shook her head vigorously. "No," she said firmly. "That's not going to happen. He can't do that." She slammed her fist onto the table, and the dishes rattled. "Goddamn it, Helen, hasn't the bastard done enough to you? He beat you up every time he got drunk, he spent every penny either of you made, he left you with nothing. Hasn't he done fucking enough?"

Helen shook her head slowly, and the tears spilled down her cheeks. "I don't know what to do. I just don't know what to do."

Woody went to Helen and cradled her in her arms. But there was nothing she could say in the way of comfort, nothing she could say at all, because the fear had come back and was just sitting there in the pit of her stomach, and she needed every ounce of strength to keep it from overwhelming her.

And now, the next day, as she lay beside Helen and held her close, Woody felt something slip in her mind. Like the edges of land at a faultline. As if a subtle shift had occurred in the landscape.

It was just a small slip, hardly noticeable really. Except that she had felt it before — a long time before. During that year she had been in the snake pit they called a mental institution. She frowned and put her hand to her temple. Or had it been yesterday?

She stared up at the ceiling, at the old water stain over the bed where the ceiling had dripped that time before the roof was fixed. As she watched, the stain became a face that glared down at her. She closed her eyes tightly and tried to keep the fear at bay.

PART
TWO

WEDNESDAY

6

SEPTEMBER

1989

It was the same nightmare.

It was always the same nightmare.

Stephanie knew the events that took place in it were not happening. They could not be happening. They already had occurred over twenty-five years ago.

Nevertheless, she had fallen asleep in her bed, passed through a murky twilight, and awakened in this terrible reality where the horror played itself out over and over again.

She was standing on the sixth floor of a dim, dusty warehouse. Crates of books lined the walls, were stacked against one another in row upon row as far as she could see in either direction. Sunlight was dirtied as it filtered through the grimy, floor-to-ceiling windows.

In slow motion, her nightmare self raised the window closest to her. It squeaked in its frame, protested the letting in of a purer light. Leaning on the windowsill, she looked out, knowing before she did so what she would see. The crisp air brushed against her face, briefly played with her hair.

Crowds lined the boulevard waiting for the horror to begin again.

To her left, up the boulevard, the motorcade was approaching, as it always did in this unreal world.

Inside the building, far to her right, in front of a window like the one she was looking out of, she knew there was a young man with a rifle.

She wanted to start the long run toward him now instead of waiting like the crowd below for what would happen in the next minutes. But her feet were rooted as firmly to the floor as if they had been nailed there.

Immobilized, powerless, she turned — for the first time, the hundredth time? — to look at the man who was such an impossible distance away.

He was drawing the bolt back.

He was moving the rifle toward the window.

Unwillingly, she turned back to look down at the street. The crowd had became noisier. The cheering had started. A boy sitting on his father's shoulders bounced up and down, holding onto the man's hair, waving a flag. Others in the crowd were craning their necks now, wanting that first glimpse of the motorcade.

The motorcade rounded the curve.

Suddenly, with a cry of intense relief, she felt her feet become less entangled with the dirty wooden floor, and she started the run — the long run that she knew even as she started it would end in a terrible defeat once more.

Her nightmare self moved through the quicksand of her terror in painful, slow-motion steps, each movement an agony of fear. She knew she could not stop what was coming, knew even as her feet struggled with the floor, knew even as she fought to do the impossible that these events could not be happening again. Still, she took each mired, anguished step as if she could somehow prevent the ancient horror this time.

Her heart pounded in her chest so loudly that it became an almost deafening sound in her ears. She passed another window and involuntarily glanced into the street.

The cheering of the crowd was a muffled drone as it reached her ears past the crashing of her heart. It sounded macabre. She hated the sound, hated the people who made it, feeling that, at least in this world where the atrocity took place time and time again, surely they knew what was coming and yet eagerly anticipated being witnesses to it again.

Still, she took each maddeningly snail-like step, hoping against all reasonable hope that this time she would not be too late.

The convertible appeared in the street below, the flags on either side of its shining hood snapping briskly in the wind.

She was too far away from the dark-haired young man with the instrument of death in his hands.

She knew she was too far away.

She was always too far away.

Her heart raced furiously now, the air in her lungs burned, and she labored for each breath as she moved through the impossible, slow-motion terror.

The barrel of the rifle glinted in the sunlight streaming through the open window.

She opened her mouth to scream, but her throat closed, refusing to utter the sound. She was close now, almost close enough to touch the rifle. She reached out, strained her arm almost out of its socket.

The young man was pressing his cheek to the stock. She saw his finger on the trigger, squeezing slowly, excruciatingly slowly. Her nerves seemed to twist and fray with the waiting for what was coming next.

The rifle discharged, firing flames into the chill air, and she knew without looking what horror was taking place in the street below. She opened her mouth, and a silent scream tore her throat.

Then he was pulling the trigger again. She saw the sunlight

glint off the metal of the trigger guard, saw the slow, careful squeeze.

Her hand touched the rifle just as it was fired, and a groan of pain escaped her lips.

The young man turned his eyes toward her.

A tear trickled down his cheek.

Stephanie awoke sitting up in bed, her body shaking and wet with perspiration. Arms were around her, holding her tightly.

"Stef, Stephanie. It's okay, sweetheart. It's okay. It's over now."

"I can't breathe," Stephanie whispered.

Marian loosened her hold slightly, and Stephanie took a huge gulp of air. She ran her fingers through her damp hair and swung her legs off the bed. "I've got to get outside."

Finding her bathrobe on the chair across the room, she shrugged into it and made her way down the hall and through the house to the screened-in porch. She sat in the swing and waited.

A moment later, Marian appeared in the doorway, tying her bathrobe around her. Stephanie watched as she brushed her fingers through her full, chestnut hair. Although she couldn't see Marian's eyes, she knew they were filled with concern.

"Was it the same one?"

"Yes."

"Any different at all?"

Stephanie shook her head.

Marian sighed. "You want some hot tea, sweetheart?"

"That would be nice."

"How about some company while I'm gone?" Marian smiled and nodded toward the sleek black cat that had pushed its head around the door frame.

Stephanie smiled. "Sure. Here, cat." She clicked her fingers near the floor, and the cat wandered across the porch, rubbed against her leg, and jumped into her lap. After a moment, it settled down to be stroked.

"You know," Marian said, "we're going to have to come up with a name sooner or later. Pretty soon, she'll believe her name's Cat, and we'll have to train her all over again."

Stephanie nodded. "We'll give it some thought."

While Marian was gone, she sat and looked out toward the street. The streetlight played through the magnolia trees and fronds of the small palms in the front yard, sifting and scattering light as the leaves played in a slight, cool breeze. There was a crispness to the air that hinted at a fall that was not too far distant.

Marian's yard, as they referred to it, since she was the one who usually decided which plants would be rooted out and where the new ones would go, would be fading soon as cooler weather approached the northeast Florida coast. In the spring, the yard around their small, shingled house in Saint Augustine took on a jungle aspect and was awash with the heavy perfume of freshly blooming magnolias and gardenias. Even through early fall, coleus and caladiums splashed among the lush greenery in brilliant and more muted colors.

The cat stirred herself and leaped lightly to the floor. Crossing to the door, she looked back at Stephanie and gave a sharp, vocal command. Stephanie laughed softly.

"You're taking over, you know," she said. "You're as bad as Mr. Pye was." Remembering the huge, fluffy orange cat who had made his life with them for so many years, she felt a twinge of sadness as she got up to let the cat out and then went back to the swing.

As she sat lost in thought, a stronger breeze wafted up from the finger of Matanzas Bay that intruded upon the land in back of their house. She took a deep breath, exhaled it slowly, and allowed the primordial fragrance of the landlocked bit of ocean to flow through her, stilling her. Whereas Marian's solace was the earth, hers was the sea.

It was one of their many differences, Stephanie thought. But from the beginning she had believed that their very differences were possibly their relationship's greatest strength. She smiled. The irony, though — and one that both of them had since realized — was that those differences might well have kept them apart before they had even met those nine years ago. Those nine good years ago. She leaned back in the swing and allowed her mind to flow back in time.

"Stef?"

Stephanie came back to the present and watched as Marian, who was standing across the porch holding two mugs, obviously repeated something.

"Sorry. What did you say?"

"I said," Marian replied, "'Do you want lemon?'"

Stephanie shook her head and smiled.

Marian cocked her head to one side and gave Stephanie an inquisitive look. "What were you thinking about?"

"Maybe I'll tell you later."

"I'll nag you until you do."

Stephanie laughed. "Don't I know it."

Handing Stephanie one of the mugs, Marian sat down beside her on the swing. "Where's your friend?"

"She seemed to have important business elsewhere."

"I told you she'd keep you company while I was gone. I suppose it's always a bad idea to promise something for somebody else, isn't it?"

Stephanie smiled again. "It would seem so."

They sipped the tea and sat in silence for several minutes before Stephanie said, "I wonder what the point of this is."

"You mean the fact that it's Kennedy's assassination all over again? Or at least it appears to be?"

"Mmm."

Marian shrugged. "Do you think it has to do with one of the Kennedys?"

"Not really, but I don't know. It could have to do with the president, or the governor of Texas, or a governor of some other state, or—" She sat the mug down on the small table beside her and fished in her pockets.

"Looking for these?" Marian reached into her pocket and held out a pack of cigarettes and a lighter.

"Thanks."

"Mmm."

"But it could have to do with anything. A person named Kennedy, someone like Lee Harvey Oswald — whether or not he did it by himself. It could have to do with Dallas—" She laughed shortly. "It could have to do with Dallas, Georgia, for all I know. There are just too many possibilities and not enough clues yet."

"But the nightmares are getting worse, aren't they?"

"More intense. In the beginning, it was — fuzzy. Now, it's very clear. I assume whatever's going to happen is getting closer in time."

"You know what I've been thinking about?"

"Once in a while," Stephanie said dryly.

Marian playfully slapped Stephanie's thigh. "You mean almost always. I'm the proverbial open book to you. All you have to do is turn the pages." She was silent for a moment. "What I keep thinking about is the nightmare repeating itself. Over and over and over. I remember the day Kennedy was killed — anyone who was old enough at the time still remembers it, of course. I was fourteen. I was home sick with the flu. My dad was at work, and my mom had gone to the drugstore to get a prescription filled. When she got home, I was sitting in bed, staring at the television. Everybody's face was so worried, then so sad."

She sat the mug down and got up. Folding her arms across her chest, she looked out at the yard. "Mom had heard it on the radio while she was out. She held me and watched it with me for a long time. I asked her why they had done it. She couldn't answer me. She just sat there and held me, and then I realized she was crying. For the next few days, she tried to shield me from it. But one day, she had to leave to get groceries, and I turned on the television again. I guess that was the first day they had the tape that actually showed the assassination. It just kept happening over and over. I don't know how many times I saw it. That night, I kept seeing it. The same way it was on television. Over and over and over again. I couldn't get it out of my mind."

"I know," Stephanie said. "I was still going to school in Boston and living at home. I sat up half the night reading, trying to shut out all the fear and anger and — excitement that was going on around me."

"Excitement?" Marian turned back to Stephanie and frowned. "You mean the upset?"

"The upset, yes. But the excitement, too. The excitement that happens when there's an accident, for instance. Or a fire. There's a fascination about it — an excitement — that draws people to watch."

There was a moment of silence, and then, more softly, Stephanie said, "Is it always going to be this way?"

"Is what always going to be this way?"

"The death, the misery." Stephanie fiddled with the ashtray and avoided looking up. "Sometimes, when I feel sorry for myself, I start thinking it follows me around rather than that I just tap into it when it's there." Although having just put out the first cigarette, she lit a fresh one and pulled in a deep breath. As she let out the smoke, she coughed slightly.

Marian rolled her eyes upward but said nothing.

"I mean, sometimes I get so tired of this. Sometimes I think if I just refused to work on any more of these cases — missing persons, murder, all of it — the visions would just stop. Maybe if I refused to do anything except readings for ordinary, everyday people, it would shut the door to all the death." She closed her eyes and leaned back in the swing.

"You know yourself that when we met," she continued, "it was manageable. It happened every couple of years. Then it was every year. Now, it seems as if one thing ends and another begins. I just get so tired sometimes."

Marian sat down and put her arms around Stephanie and held her close, hearing the break in Stephanie's voice, knowing that tears for her were rare and that they were very close now. She rocked her gently. "I don't know what to tell you, sweetheart. I just don't know. But you're not alone, you know."

"I know." Stephanie's voice was muffled against Marian's shoulder.

They sat quietly for a while. The sky began to pinken.

"The sun's coming up," Marian said. She felt Stephanie nod against her shoulder. "You feel up to a huge breakfast at the Lighthouse? Scrambled eggs, crisp bacon, grits, maybe an English muffin?"

Stephanie leaned back and raised an eyebrow. "Food cures everything?"

"Indubitably. It's my Italian mama's training, remember?" She grinned. "We're on?"

"We're on." Stephanie smiled.

When Stephanie left to change clothes, Marian sat in the swing for a moment, looking out at the yard. Stephanie's question kept pounding at her: Is it always going to be this way? It tore Stephanie apart and disrupted their lives from time to time. And it had even brought a psychotic killer into their home the last time, just a few short months ago. It was that murderer, originally bent on revenge against Stephanie for putting him in prison, who had killed Mr. Pye, the orange cat they had loved so much. The image of opening the door and seeing the hideous mutilation was one which she had a hard time keeping from her mind when she thought of Mr. Pye and his trusting gentleness. The terror that had been visited on them by that psychotic hatred and rage was something they were still trying to shake.

And it was that murderer who had raped her.

She sighed and put her hand on her stomach. But Stephanie's involvement in the case had, in a sense, also given them their child — the child she carried inside of her whose father was now dead. It had been a difficult decision whether to continue the pregnancy when they discovered the "morning-after pill" had not worked, and some of the reasons for that decision were still not clear to her. They had come from her heart, though, not from her head — she knew that. She also knew that they had very much to do with her love for Stephanie. For now, that was enough.

She sighed. She had hoped Stephanie wouldn't have something else on her mind, distracting her, until the baby was born.

But now, these nightmares had begun a couple of weeks ago. And nightmares, for Stephanie, almost always meant her involvement in yet another incident of violence, whether past or future.

Stephanie appeared in the doorway, and Marian looked up.

"Don't worry about the baby," Stephanie said quietly. "Everything's going to be all right. I'll be with you."

Marian smiled. She arose, went into Stephanie's arms, and was held closely, lovingly. After a moment, though, hearing Stephanie chuckle against her ear, she pulled back and looked at her. "And just what is that about?"

"Well, you know when you came out here with the tea, you asked me what I'd been thinking?"

"Mmm."

"What I was thinking about was when we met. And the next morning, when we went to breakfast at the Lighthouse. Remember?"

"You think I could forget?"

"Did I ever tell you how Karen got me to come to her party?"

Marian laughed. "Some form of extortion was mentioned, I believe." She poked Stephanie in the ribs. "So, maybe at breakfast we'll reminisce? Get our minds off unpleasant things?"

Stephanie nodded, her eyes sad for a moment. "I'm really sorry."

Marian lifted an eyebrow. "What for, sweetheart?"

Stephanie shrugged. "I don't know. For all of it, I guess. Sometimes I think that if we'd never met, you wouldn't have had so much pain, that—"

Marian frowned and put her fingers across Stephanie's lips. "Don't you dare *ever* say that again, you hear me?" She stared into Stephanie's eyes and touched her fingertips to Stephanie's cheek, where the jagged scar lay. Stephanie had a too-strong sense of responsibility, a tendency to be overwhelmed by guilt at every turn. It had probably started the day she acquired that scar. But it seemed to have left an even deeper scar on Stephanie's soul.

"You hear me?" Marian whispered more intently. "All the love we've had together — all the joy you've given me — far outweighs any pain. You must know that."

Stephanie said nothing for a moment, and then she gave Marian a small smile and nodded her head. "Yes," she whispered in response. "I do." She took Marian in her arms once more and held her for a long time before she could let her go.

THURSDAY

7

SEPTEMBER

1989

Mary Fowler turned over and found that she was alone in bed. She propped herself on one elbow and looked at the clock on the dresser. Six-thirty. She frowned and threw back the covers.

It had been so hot the summer of '88 that at times she had wondered if it would ever be cool again. That year, Georgia had been hard hit by the drought that had covered most of the country, and their crops had suffered terribly. Now, this summer, it had seemed to rain most of the time, and they were going into the fall with well over ten inches above normal rainfall. The lake levels were way up, and they had had to concern themselves more with making sure the crops didn't rot in the fields than with whether they would dry up.

She went to the closet, pulled out a robe, and slid her feet into the slippers George had bought her last Christmas — the ones with the little Garfields staring up at her. She wiggled her toes and smiled. When she had protested that she was too old for such foolishness, George just grinned. "The little bit of silver in your hair don't mean you're old, darlin'. It just means you're more beautiful to me than ever." And that had closed the subject.

Smelling coffee, she shuffled off to the kitchen. As she passed the dining room, she saw George sitting at the table, staring out of the full-length glass doors across the field closest to the house. She smiled again. His hair, still heavy and dark even in his late forties, although it had begun thinning a bit in the past year, stuck up in the morning much like Alfalfa's on "The Little Rascals." She stood in the doorway for a moment, watching him.

"Planting next year's crop so soon?"

She heard him chuckle softly.

"Maybe."

Coming up from behind, she put her arms around him and kissed the top of his head. "You want some coffee? You made it."

He snorted. "Maybe it won't be too bad this time."

"Maybe, but I wouldn't count on it."

As she started to withdraw her arms, he caught her hand and kissed the palm. "I love you," he whispered.

She smiled and ruffled his hair. "You just want me to make fresh coffee."

When Mary had left the room, George Fowler sighed and closed his eyes tightly. After the nightmares he had been having, his head always felt as if it were splitting from the pain. He had said nothing to Mary. There was nothing she could do, and he felt the nightmares would go away soon — as soon as he knew whether the governor would be appointing him to the Georgia House of Representatives.

He opened his eyes. He should have told Mary about the nightmares, but he didn't want her to worry along with him. He hadn't even told her about the possible appointment. Probably worse still, he hadn't told her that Henry Cutchner, now seventy-eight years old, a man their families had known for twenty years, lay dying in a hospital in Atlanta.

The governor had called him a week ago about taking Henry's place in the House. The nightmares had begun the next night.

He felt that he was holding a lonely, macabre vigil over a dying man — not wanting him to die yet, knowing that only through Cutchner's death would he be appointed to the legislature. And he was in turmoil even about that. He was a farmer; maybe he was meant to be a farmer all his life. Of course, there were those who would more aptly call him a small businessman; his farm was more than a little successful.

He and Mary had suffered through long, hard years when the farm wavered on the brink of disaster. At times he had lain awake long after Mary had fallen asleep in his arms, worrying about whether he would be able to put food on the table the next day for her and their four children. He saw when she gave him and the kids what meat there was on the platter, protesting that she was watching her weight when he knew it was not true. Hurting over that, he had decided to get a regular, paying job, but Mary would not hear of it. He was a farmer, she had said, and she believed he could make the farm pay.

And she had been right. Finally, one year had been good, and then the two after that. The land had begun paying for itself. At first, it was just a little, but then it had snowballed as he had found more markets for his crops. And Mary's idea about raising chickens to sell instead of just for their own use had been right on the money, too. When they signed the contract to sell all the chickens they could produce to that big poultry outfit, they were virtually assured of success. Soon, they had begun building their dream house, and their lives since then had been secure and happy.

He smiled. Their lives, even through the lean years, had been happy. Mary had made them so. And even though Mary persisted in saying that he had given their family what they had today, he knew the truth about it. Without Mary, he believed in his heart, they would have had nothing. No, more than that, he thought. He would have *been* nothing.

He went to the window and stood looking out. He rubbed at his temples. The nightmare had been even worse last night. It had awakened him before dawn, a headache splitting his head from side to side. And he couldn't even remember what the nightmare was about.

The only memory he carried with him into the morning was a flash of fire high above his head. And the sound of Mary screaming.

Hearing Mary call him from the kitchen, he turned. He had loved her as a young girl — she had been only seventeen when they married; he had been barely eighteen — and now, almost thirty years later, he loved her even more than on their wedding day. Sometimes when he looked at her, he thought she had never aged a day. Sometimes when he lay beside her at night and couldn't go to sleep right away, his heart felt so full of his love for her that it almost ached.

He breathed deeply and tried to relax. The headache was abating. Hearing Mary call out that his breakfast was going to go to the pigs if he didn't hurry up, he smiled and headed for the kitchen.

THURSDAY

7

SEPTEMBER

1989

Helen finished rinsing the last glass from the lunch dishes, turned off the water, and reached for the dishtowel lying on the counter beside the sink. She dried her hands, spread the towel on the rack inside the cabinet below, and left the door open so the towel would dry.

At least Atlanta's suffocating humidity had lessened in the past few days as a front of cooler air had passed through the lower South. During the hottest months, when the temperature and humidity had combined to make their second-story, non-air-conditioned apartment miserable, she had had to wash clothes twice as often just to keep the towels from souring. The dishtowel was slightly askew, and she straightened it with meticulous care before she realized why she was spending so much time on the dish-washing chore.

She was avoiding Woody. She sighed heavily, pushed a dark blonde strand of hair out of her eyes, and looked toward the door that led to the living room. Woody was in there, she knew, but she had heard nothing for the past hour. That was not like the Woody she had begun living with more than three years ago.

Helen smiled slightly, remembering the years when she and Woody and Katie had all been together. There had always been noise then — sometimes ear-splitting shrieks from Katie as Woody played with her, sometimes even louder shrieks from Woody as Katie tickled her and Woody pretended that Katie was getting the best of her. Sometimes Helen felt she had been the mother of them both.

And even when Woody was alone with her, when Katie was visiting the next-door neighbor's boy, Woody made noise. She never did anything quietly, Helen had thought then, and sometimes it had been annoying, particularly when Helen wanted to get Katie out from under foot for a couple of hours to get some peace and quiet. No matter what Woody did, she was always humming or talking loudly to herself or banging things around.

Helen looked toward the door again. For months now, Woody had been quiet. Quieter even than the day the court had taken Katie away from them. Even when she was talking to herself, she was quiet. In fact, she looked as if she were talking to someone else.

She felt tears spring to her eyes unexpectedly, and she brushed them away with the back of her hand. It had been hard enough to lose Katie. Now, she felt as if she were losing Woody, too.

She took a deep breath, released it, and resolutely entered the living room.

Woody was in the window seat across the room, one knee on the seat and the other foot braced against the floor. She looked as if she were aiming a rifle out the casement window, but she had nothing in her hands.

Puzzled, Helen watched her for a moment before she spoke. "What are you doing?"

There was a long silence, and then Woody's voice was muffled. "The bastards deserve to die."

Realizing so suddenly that it took her breath away that Woody had been doing exactly what it had looked like, Helen lowered herself into the worn, overstuffed armchair, her knees weakened as if they had been replaced by warm jelly. She studied her lover across the living room and tried to keep her voice calm, even though her throat was tight with apprehension. She felt she had been waiting for this.

"Which ones, Woody?"

"The ones who took Katie from us."

"You mean Doug? Or his parents? Or the judge and jury at the trial? Who would you start with?"

Woody shifted her position on the window seat and lowered the invisible rifle, but she did not turn away from the window.

"It's society who took her from us," Helen said, her words sounding too loud for the small, quiet room. "It's society that said I'm an unfit mother because I love you. It's society that said there's something wrong — something dangerous — about a little girl living with two women who love each other." She took a deep, shuddering breath. With as much suddenness as the fear had come, it left and was replaced by the bone-deep weariness that nagged at her so often these days. And then she said the only thing that was in her mind.

"You'd have to kill most of the world, Woody," she said softly. "And where in God's name would you start?"

She got up and walked slowly to the door. "This is crazy. In the first place, I don't think you can kill anyone." She saw Woody's back stiffen.

In times past, she thought, when Woody was troubled about something, she would have gone to her, wrapped her arms around her. This time, it was as if Woody had pulled a wall hard around herself — a wall tall enough and thick enough and so well locked that there was no getting through it.

She wanted to say for maybe the thousandth time, "Hey, sweetheart, we'll make it. It'll be okay." She wanted to say those reassuring words again, but somehow she couldn't make herself utter them. Not this time. This time, she felt if she said them, they would be a lie. Because this time, she herself did not believe them.

For a long time after she heard Helen leave the room, Woody continued to stare out the window. She toyed with a flaking bit of white paint on the window frame, scratched at it with her fingernail until it fell off and drifted down in the slight breeze.

The leaves on the huge oak tree near the second-story window turned vein-side up in a gust of cooler air. The faint metallic smell of imminent rain drifted in the window. She stared into the distance, past the tops of trees that would take on a golden red tinge soon, and watched as the sky seemed to turn an angry black over the Atlanta skyline.

Her eyes were caught by a shaft of sunlight that pierced the coming storm clouds and gleamed on the tiny-looking gold dome of the Georgia State Capitol.

Helen was right about one thing, of course. Society was to blame. And she couldn't kill society.

She toyed with another fleck of paint and watched as it blew away from the window ledge. What she was going to have to do was find that part of society that was infecting the rest of it.

She frowned. But was Helen right about the rest of it? Was it impossible for her to kill?

A Volkswagen Cabriolet pulled up to the nearby traffic light. She lifted the rifle again to her shoulder and snuggled her cheek against the smooth, cool, wooden stock. She sighted down the barrel, through the telescopic sight, and saw the back of the driver's head come into close view. His blond hair was ruffling in the slight breeze. As he lifted his right hand from the steering wheel, she centered the cross hairs on the back of his neck and squeezed the trigger. An ugly hole opened in the man's neck, sprayed blood and bone and flesh against the windshield, and he slumped forward over the wheel. The horn blared in the silence down in the street.

She continued to look through the sight and felt her stomach lurch, but she controlled it with effort. She lifted her head from the rifle, and after a minute, when her stomach had quieted, she felt satisfied, reassured.

A moment later, the young blond man in the car brushed his fingers through his hair and drove off.

Woody frowned and looked down in puzzlement at her hands. There was no gun there.

It took her a few seconds to remember. There were times when she felt she had been dropped down that old, bottomless black hole. Sometimes she felt that she had to claw her way out, up a slick, glassy side, but she never made it quite to the top. At first, she had tried very hard to climb out, but after a while, it had become more and more difficult, and it seemed easier to stay at the bottom. It was dark there, but it was safe.

Of course, the voice was down there with her, too. Sometimes she didn't like that. Sometimes she just wanted to be alone. Alone with her own thoughts instead of the mixture of her thoughts and the thoughts of the voice.

She stared out of the window.

She would have to get a gun. A rifle.

The dome of the Capitol building caught her eye again. *You'd have to kill the whole world,* Helen had said. But Helen was wrong, Woody considered. Her eyes narrowed as she looked at the gold glinting in the overcast sun.

She wouldn't have to kill the whole world.

Not at all.

She would just have to destroy the cancer that was eating away at the world.

She picked up the rifle and the cleaning cloth from the window ledge. Cradling the rifle across her knees, she began polishing it, running the cloth over the stock, down the barrel, back over the stock, and then over the barrel once more. Her lips moved soundlessly, while the room darkened with the storm's approach.

1

"It's dead."

"I refuse to accept that judgment," Stephanie replied firmly. "It's merely resting."

"Resting, my ass. If it were a horse, we'd have to shoot it to put it out of its misery."

Stephanie tried to keep her face composed at this last jibe, but the grin finally won out. She leaned over and whispered to the faded red paint on the '74 VW's fender, "Don't listen to her. All you need is a good tune-up. That's all."

Marian laughed shortly, then she saw Stephanie's look of mock hurt and sighed in resignation. "What did the mechanic say?"

"What do mechanics know? Most of them don't even have souls."

"Christ," Marian groaned softly. She put her hand over her eyes, rubbed them, and sighed again. Finally, she smiled brightly at Stephanie. "Well, dear, if it's what you want." She turned and walked toward the house.

Stephanie frowned briefly and then chuckled. "Hey, lady, are you patronizing me?"

Marian stopped dead in her tracks, swung around, and rested her hand on her hip. She smiled. "You bet your sweet ass I am."

Stephanie laughed softly as Marian turned and walked away again. As she watched her mount the front steps to the porch, she took in Marian's bare, tanned legs, the white, getting-too-tight shorts, and the smooth bare back under the halter. She watched Marian's slow, languid movements, the ample hips and thighs, and a quite sudden sensual ache made itself known.

With infinite care, she sent her mind out. *Marian?* she whispered mentally. She surrounded her lover with her touch, her mouth on the back of her neck, her palms gliding down the warm long legs and back up and between the silky thighs. She saw Marian stop abruptly just as she opened the screen door. She turned, and Stephanie felt her draw in and release a deep breath. She withdrew her mind carefully, tenderly.

Marian raised a questioning eyebrow, and then a slow smile started across her mouth, and she held her hand out toward Stephanie. As Stephanie reached her, she said softly, "After all these years — how many did we decide it was?"

"Close to nine, I believe."

"Well, after nine years, you can still do that to me, can't you?"

"I still want you. I always will."

Marian placed her hands on Stephanie's shoulders and pulled her close. She ran her fingers through the hair at the nape of Stephanie's neck and tugged at it slightly, just enough so her head was pulled back and Marian could look into her eyes.

"You want a very pregnant lady?"

"I want you," Stephanie whispered.

Marian lifted an eyebrow again. "And how about the stretch marks later?"

"I will always want you."

"That's what they all say." Marian laughed, and she pulled Stephanie across the porch. "Well, just in case you change your mind, I guess I should get it while I can." She grinned as she heard Stephanie laugh behind her.

"I really should quit smoking, I suppose." Stephanie eyed the glowing tip of the cigarette she held in her right hand while Marian snuggled closer on her left shoulder. She ran her hand down to Marian's ribs and patted the warm skin.

Marian took in a small, sharp breath. "I'm still sensitive, dear. If you don't want to start me up again, I suggest you don't touch me like that." She smiled at Stephanie's chuckle. "By the way—" She hugged Stephanie closer. "Because of the baby?"

"Well, it would be for you, too."

"And not for you? I mean, there seems to be a lack of conclusive evidence these days about secondhand smoke. It looks like it's a problem for children, possibly because their immune systems are not yet fully developed, but nobody's been able to prove that most adults are bothered by it any more than by the increased pollution we're subjected to. We can keep the baby away from it, so if you want to quit, do it for yourself."

Stephanie shrugged. "I know I should, but without the incentive outside of myself, I probably wouldn't think about it."

"Then it probably won't work."

"You're probably right." She sighed and reached over to the night table beside the bed and tapped ashes off the cigarette.

"You know," Marian said, snuggling down further against Stephanie, "not to change the subject, but I got into a discussion with Leona the Straight a couple of days ago. On the subject of feminist politics, of course."

"Again?" Stephanie grinned. "You know, it's not very sisterly of us to call her that."

"I wouldn't call her that if she didn't keep saying it herself. You can't have a conversation with the woman without her making sure you know she's totally heterosexual. In fact, I often wonder if she protests just a bit too much."

"I know. It does make you wonder, doesn't it? Well, anyway, can I assume you managed to control yourself this time?"

"Admirably."

"Why does the smile on your face lead me to believe otherwise?"

Marian's smile gave way to a laugh. "You're terrible. If it were up to you, I'd never have any fun."

"Right. And what was today's conversation about? Or do I want to know?"

"Oh, I suspect you'd be interested. It was about so-called sadomasochistic tendencies in women who consider themselves to be feminists."

"Uh-oh."

Marian poked Stephanie in the side. "Actually, I didn't say very much."

Stephanie lifted an eyebrow. "I'll bet."

Marian poked Stephanie harder and laughed again. "Well, she was ranting and raving about where all those horrible, politically incorrect tendencies come from." She ticked them off on her fingers. "Capitalistic, imperialistic, male-dominated societies. If we were all truly free, sayeth Leona, we would have no tendency at all to want to be dominated in bed." She took a deep breath. "So, of course, I said I thought all she needed was a good fuck with a good woman."

"You didn't say that!"

"No. But I thought it." Marian shook her head. "God, that *is* terrible, isn't it?"

"Don't be too hard on yourself. Leona seems to elicit that kind of response from a lot of us. So what did you really say?"

"I said I thought that was what she believed about women being lesbians."

"I seem to recall her saying that one time."

"She *did* say it."

"And then she said," Stephanie prompted.

"And then she said that it was true. The two are exactly the same. If we hadn't been born into a capitalistic, imperialistic, etcetera, etcetera, society, then none of us would be lesbians, or homosexuals, or have any sexual perversions at all." Marian gave Stephanie a mock-sage look. "By the way, did you realize that there are no gays or lesbians in Red China? At least in the early seventies, there weren't."

Stephanie's eyebrows raised a bit. "Oh?"

Marian nodded emphatically. "Indeed. I had a friend who lived in New York for a while back then, and she called the embassy there and asked what the gay population was. She was told there wasn't one."

"Oh," Stephanie said, grinning.

"Mmm. I thought that was incredibly interesting, also. Well, back to Leona, concerning the fact that all of those terrible perversions are caused by all those other things I just enumerated, I told her I thought that was bullshit."

"You really did?"

"Yep. She ignored it, though."

"May I assume that you didn't let it go at that?"

"I told her that lesbians are born, not made. Unless they want to be."

Stephanie howled and pounded lightly on Marian's hip in her glee. "You're kidding! You didn't!"

"Yes." She gave Stephanie a mock-wounded look. "You seem not to believe me. And then I brought the conversation back to the issue of why some women like to be dominated in bed."

"Oh?"

"Yeah." Marian rubbed circles on Stephanie's stomach. "I told her I had decided that it was the same thing as being a lesbian. When I was growing up, I didn't make a decision to be attracted to women, that I only made a decision later to act on it. But when I was touched by a woman I was attracted to, conscious decision had nothing to do with the fact that my body tingled all over and I started getting wet between my legs—"

"You didn't say that!"

"No. At least not in those words. But I said most of it. I also said I don't decide to get turned on when you hold me down and make love to me a little roughly sometimes, either. My body reacts, and that reaction comes from my head, of course, but I don't make a conscious decision to turn on. And I believe it's similar to my being a lesbian. It's part of me. Period. I'd stopped worrying about being a lesbian or how that happened, and I'd also stopped worrying about my sometimes so-called masochistic tendencies, too."

"And what was her response to that revelation?"

"I don't think she believed me. I've put her on before about too many other things. She doesn't know what to believe now."

Realizing that Stephanie had become very quiet, Marian glanced at her face. Her jaw was clenched, and it made the scar more prominent. "What's wrong?"

Stephanie's voice was faint. "I don't know. It feels as if something were rushing at me. Something with a lot of fear behind it."

The shrill ring of the telephone caused them both to jump. Stephanie's face went blank for a moment, and then she closed her eyes and took a deep breath. She looked at Marian wistfully. "I think it's the beginning," she whispered. She bent over, kissed Marian lightly on the mouth, and reached for the telephone on Marian's side of the bed.

A few minutes later, she hung up the receiver and swung her legs over the side of the bed.

"Bad news?"

Stephanie shrugged slightly. "Not right away, I don't think. But I've got a feeling it may be bad pretty soon. Would you like to go to Atlanta for a few days? See some old friends? That was Corky inviting us up for the weekend — or longer, if we want to stay."

"That might be nice. Can we leave in the morning, or do you have clients?"

"I only have three tomorrow. I may be able to see one tonight, and the other two won't mind waiting." She found her t-shirt on the floor beside the bed and pulled it on. "I'll call."

"You mind if I sit down here?"

Woody had been lost in thought and started at the older woman's soft voice. She looked up. "No, of course not." She slid to one side of the concrete bench and heard the woman sigh as she sat, saw the small wince of pain.

The woman smiled almost apologetically. "My hip's been bothering me with all the rain we been havin'. The dampness just seems to get into my bones. Later in the fall, rain or not, it settles in for the winter." She adjusted her skirt. "I try not to complain too much, but I've been walking a lot today, and it's worse."

Woody smiled back at her, thinking that it would be hard not to. She remembered what a friend had said once when someone asked what she thought God looked like. "God is a sixty-year-old, wonderfully fat, black woman," the friend had said. "And She makes iced tea so strong and sweet that you just know She's from the South." This woman, Woody considered, would have fit the description, whether or not she made iced tea the same way. She continued to smile and looked back at the gold dome rising so high above them across Washington Street that her neck was starting to ache.

"It's something, isn't it?" the woman said.

Woody nodded.

"My son says when he walks from the bus stop every morning, he stands here for a minute just to look at it."

"Your son?"

"He's a guard at the Capitol. The top one, I guess you'd say."

Woody nodded again. The woman had said it with a great deal of pride. It was something to think about. She hadn't really considered it before. How many guards were there? She would have to find out. So far, the idea was very vague in her mind about how she would do what she needed to do. Now there were guards to consider.

Her head felt light, and she rubbed her eyes. She had been wandering off again. All of a sudden, she became aware that the woman had been talking to her. For how long? Time seemed to race ahead sometimes, and then sometimes she would seem to sit for hours and only a few minutes would have passed.

"—and so, he took a course at that school where they teach you how to be a security guard. It cost a good bit, of course. But nothin' that's worth anything ever comes cheap, does it?"

Woody frowned slightly. "No, I don't suppose it does." She looked back up at the dome. No, anything that was worth anything always cost something.

But sometimes it's worth paying the price, the voice said.

She heard the woman speaking again, breaking through the jumble of thoughts. How long had it been this time? Wool gathering, her mother used to call it. Maybe that was all it was. Just wool gathering. Except that it seemed to happen so much of the time now. The walls of the hole seemed glassy, more slippery than ever. She tried to concentrate harder on what the woman was saying.

"—a big mass of flowers just all over the place in the spring and summer, but they'll be putting in the fall flowers soon, of course." She nodded across the four-lane street toward the statue of a man standing beside a woman seated in a gigantic chair on the Capitol lawn. "That's Joseph Emerson Brown there and his wife, Elizabeth Grisham Brown. He was a governor, you know, right around the time of the war between the South and the North. And over there," she said, pointing to another huge bronze statue, "is Richard B. Russell. He was a governor during most of the Great Depression and a United States senator and—" She chuckled and reached over to pat Woody's knee. "Just listen to me, going on and on, just like I know all there is to know about it."

"You know a lot more than I do," Woody said.

The woman smiled. "I guess it's sort of like livin' in New York City in a way. I hear that folks who live there see the Statue of Liberty every day and most of them probably don't ever go visit it. You just sort of take things for granted when they're always there."

"I suppose."

The woman turned slightly. "That bell there—"

Woody swiveled to look at the Liberty Bell replica that rested on a stand behind them.

"They rang that last year when the Capitol was a hundred years old." She turned back to face the Capitol. "Just to look at it, you wouldn't think it was a hundred years old, would you?"

"No, I guess not."

"You know, when they first built the Capitol, they brought the gold all the way from Dahlonega in wagons pulled by horses. Of course, it don't — doesn't look that old, because they put the new gold over the top of it in 1981. They brought that by wagons, too. Just to show how they did it the first time."

"I remember seeing the scaffolding when they were working on it."

The woman nodded. "You know, folks all over Georgia gave money to put gold on that dome. And lots of schoolchildren, too — some just gave nickels and dimes, but all of it helped make it look so pretty again." She shook her head with a smile. "There I go again." She sighed and lifted her head to look up at the dome, and her voice was softer. "I guess I just think it's a mighty powerful-looking thing."

Woody frowned. "It is powerful," she said. "Maybe too powerful."

"How do you mean?"

Woody shrugged. "Nothing."

The woman waited a minute and then said, "I come here sometimes around lunchtime, and my son takes me to get a bite to eat if he can get away for a little while. And if he can't, sometimes I go sit up in the gallery for a while if the General Assembly's in session like it is now. The governor called it to get them to talk about—" She paused, frowning. "I think he said it's about taxing pensions for state employees. Something like that. She laughed softly. "Lord, sometimes those men sure is—" She stopped. "Sure are funny." She glanced at Woody. "I've been taking a course at church lately. This nice woman comes and teaches us how to speak right." She chuckled. "I'm still not very good at it. I spent a lot of years not talking right. But I'm getting better. It makes me feel — younger somehow. As long as I'm learning, I'm making my life better."

Woody studied her for a moment. "You watch the General Assembly in session?"

"I sure do. The Senate sometimes, but the House a bit more. That's where they introduce most of the bills, and some of the things they come up with, child, you wouldn't hardly believe. I kind of enjoy it, even though they surely talk in circles sometimes." She laughed out loud. "They be tryin' so hard to be serious sometimes." She stopped again and shook her head. "You know, it's hard to change the way you talk. You hear it for so many long years, it just becomes part of you."

"I don't see anything wrong with the way you talk. Why do you want to change it?"

"Well, I guess because I'd like to sound a little more like an educated woman. I think it's up to each of us to do what we can to better ourselves."

"Why is the way somebody else talks better than the way you talk?" Woody frowned. It was a subject she had wrestled with for a long time. "I mean, if you say something, and anybody who speaks English can understand you, then what difference does it make how you express yourself? Aren't you just concerned about fitting into society?" She looked at the woman. "And it's a society you didn't choose for yourself in the first place. So why do you care what some white businessman walking down the street thinks about the way you talk?"

The woman's face mirrored the frown on Woody's. "Well, I don't know that I care what he thinks about me unless I go into the bank he works in, and I try to get a loan. Now if I do that, then I know that he's going to be looking at me a little differently. And if I can speak correctly, then he might get a better impression of me." She shook her head and said softly, "It might not be right for him to judge me from the way I talk, child, but that's the way the world is, you know."

Woody stopped herself from making a sarcastic comment. The woman was obviously pleased at what she had accomplished. "Well, I think you're doing very well. You sound very educated, actually."

The woman chuckled. "Well, I don't think they're gonna be handing me any college degrees right away, but I suppose I'm doing all right."

"Do you do it often?"

"Do what, child?"

"Go up to the gallery."

"Sure. Especially when the governor talks."

Woody frowned. "The governor?"

"Mmm. You know, we got the Senate and the House of Representatives — both of them together make up the General Assembly, like the Congress for the whole country. So they all come together in the place where the House does their business to hear the governor talk. He gets up there and tells everybody how good everything is since he's been in office. It's called the State of the State address. You know, like the State of the Union that the president does, only it's for the state. How things have been so good and all." She chuckled. "Lord, he's better'n all the rest put together. He talks in circles from the time he gets up there till the time he leaves. And all of 'em are the same. Or at least I think they are. I've only been coming here for the past three of them, but so far they sound about the same."

"When does he do that?"

"Oh, it's a while now, I think. Maybe — mmm — I guess it's about the middle — no, a little earlier in January. The General Assembly's gonna finish this business, and then they'll start up again the second Monday in January. The governor comes in and gives his address sometime that week usually."

Woody stared at the gold dome. In her mind, there was a light dawning somewhere. Everything had been a field of black before, and now there was a pinpoint of light, up there in the upper left-hand corner.

"Can anyone go up there?"

"The gallery? Why, of course, baby." She paused. "Have you ever been in the Capitol?"

Woody shook her head.

"Well, you have to get a pass when you go in the front door, but that's easy to do. They'll want you to prove who you are, and they put your name on the list, but that's all there is to it. Anybody can do it. It's a free country."

Woody snorted, and she saw the woman frown. "You don't really believe it's a free country, do you? You, above all people, should know it's not."

"Me? You mean because I'm black? Child, it's a lot better now than it used to be. My great-grandmother was born a slave. She was still a little bitty thing before that war started, but she used to sit me on her knee when I was a child and tell me about what she remembered and what her mother before her remembered about that time. Why, it used to be when I was a young woman, I couldn't even eat at Woolworth's with the white folks. We be sitting at—" She hesitated. "We had to sit at the end of the counter then. Had a white and colored water fountain, too. We couldn't drink out of the white folks' water fountain. Now, that's all changed."

"Not everything's changed."

"No. Not everything. But someday. Someday it will. I believe what Dr. King said."

"And they killed him."

"Who's 'they,' child? Some man with a lot of hate in his heart did it, that's who. Hate can do some terrible things."

Not wanting to be disrespectful, Woody turned back to stare at the steps leading up to the front door of the Capitol.

"What's this country done to you to make you so bitter?"

The woman's voice had been soft. Woody looked at her. "I don't think you'd understand."

"Well, if you don't give me a chance, you'll never know, will you?"

Woody considered this for a moment. At this point, was there anything else to lose? Katie was gone. She could hardly see Helen any more, for some reason. Maybe it was that black hole with the slippery sides that she seemed to slip into so much of the time. Maybe it was the voice that kept coming at her, keeping her awake so that she felt tired all the time.

"I live with a woman who has a little girl. This great country — and this state — was so scared about our loving each other that it took her child away from her. Away from us."

"Did you hurt her in any way?"

Woody felt the rage begin to build in her chest, pound at her head. She clenched her fists, and with difficulty, she held onto the anger, tried to control it. After what seemed like hours, she spoke again.

"I never hurt her. *Never.* I loved her. I still do, but they won't let me see her."

"Then it's not right they took her."

Woody felt the anger fall away as if it had never been there. "Well, they did it anyway. That's what this great country did."

"I never said there's no wrongs done here. No, sir. There's plenty of wrongs done, baby. But I'm saying it's better. And it'll get better every day."

Woody stared at the Capitol. "Not soon enough," Woody murmured. "It won't be soon enough. There's a cancer eating away at society. I'm going to have to cut it out."

After a few minutes, Woody realized she had been rambling for a while. She sensed the woman was watching her. She turned and looked at her. The woman was frowning. There was something dangerous about this. About the way she had been talking. She didn't know what she had said. She smiled.

"I'm sorry. I just get wound up sometimes and mad about it. Everything's going to be all right. You're right, of course, someday things'll be better." She stood up. The woman was still watching her. "It was very nice meeting you. You take care of yourself, hear?"

"Sure," the woman said, smiling slightly now. "And you take care of yourself."

Woody walked to the edge of Plaza Park and turned just before she came to the corner of Washington Street and Trinity Avenue. The woman was looking in her direction. She smiled broadly and waved to her. The woman lifted her hand and gave a small wave in return.

"There's a lot of crazy people in the world, Mama. You can't lock 'em all up, and especially if they ain't done nothin' except talk."

"Haven't done anything."

Ezrah Palmer frowned and looked at his mother. "What?"

"Haven't done anything except talk. Not ain't or nothing."

Ezrah grinned. "Right, Mama. Anyway, you can't lock up all the crazies. There's too many of 'em."

"I said nothing about locking her up," Mabel Palmer said as she set a plate in front of him. "I just think there's something strange going on in that poor child's head, that's all. And it worries me somehow." She frowned. "I don't really know why. But she kept asking me all these questions about watching the General Assembly and all."

"Maybe she's just curious, Mama."

"And then," she said, pointing the cooking spoon at her son, "she started talking on and on about how she had to take care of some cancer or something. Let me tell you, Ezrah, she wasn't talking about no cancer in somebody's body, she was talking about something that—"

He held up his hand in a gesture of surrender. "Okay," he said, smiling sympathetically, "but you just worry yourself about too many things. And you don't need to do that. You need to take care of yourself. Remember what the doctor said. Don't be getting yourself so upset over nothing all the time."

Mabel snorted. "That doctor's been tellin' me the same damn thing for twenty years. There's nothing wrong with me."

He glanced up in surprise. He could probably count on the fingers of one hand how many times his mother had used a swear word in his life. "Your heart, Mama." He took a piece of bread from the plate in front of him and buttered it lavishly.

"Don't be talking to me about my heart. Look at you. You can't eat a meal without all that stuff."

"I'm still young, Mama."

"Well, young or not, you ought to be doing something about all that cholesterol."

"I know, Mama." He waved the fork at her. "But we were talking about your health."

"I'm fine." She turned to the stove and stirred the broth around the roast, then lifted the spoon to her mouth and gingerly took a sip. "All I'm saying, Ezrah, is that something's just not quite right. Once in a while, when I was talking to her, she'd be sitting there, her mouth moving like she was talking to somebody else." She pointed the spoon at him. "Only she wasn't making a sound." She frowned and put the spoon back into the pot. "Not a sound."

"What do you think she might do?"

"I don't know. Maybe nothing. I've just got a strange feeling, that's all."

"So what is it you want me to do?"

Mabel sighed and turned to look at him. "I don't guess there's anything you can do. But if you see her, just pay attention, you hear?"

Ezrah smiled. "I hear, Mama. Now, can I get some of that, or are you gonna starve me tonight?"

Mabel harrumphed in mock irritation and reached for a platter to put the roast on.

1

"I think your car could use a tune-up, too," Stephanie said. "I mean, I know it's in incredible shape, inside and out, but—"

"Too?" Marian chuckled and shook her head. "Dear, you and I both know your little car needs considerably more than a tune-up." She took a swallow of Coke and handed the bottle to Stephanie.

"Maybe, maybe not," Stephanie responded. She took the steering wheel of the '73 Buick LeSabre with her left hand so she could reach for the bottle.

Marian sighed. "Okay. So you take it in and get it a tune-up, and then we'll see if it needs anything else." She paused and then murmured, "Like maybe a new engine."

"Traitor," Stephanie growled.

"No, I just don't want you traveling all over the countryside in a car I don't know is going to get you home every time, that's all."

"You haven't been able to get rid of me yet."

"And I'm not ready to." Marian smiled. "When you get old and feeble, I'll toss you out."

Stephanie guffawed and handed the Coke back.

The Georgia State Line sign flashed by on Interstate 75 North.

2

George Fowler took off his glasses and laid them on the desk, then he leaned back in the swivel chair and rubbed his eyes. It seemed as though the paperwork took up more and more of his time. It was no wonder that smaller farmers were going under each year. They were probably being buried by paper, he thought with irritation.

He stood and went to the window, then looked out over the fields that he could see from his home office. He spied Joseph on the tractor, bouncing across the field closest to the house, a little dust cloud following him. He was going to let the field rest this coming year, graze the herd on it, and build up the soil again.

"Is your mouth already watering for Edie's fried chicken?"

George turned and found Mary, smiling, standing in the doorway. He smiled in return. "If it's fried chicken, it must be Saturday. Does that woman not know how to fix anything on different days?"

"Oh, I don't know. You may like a little more excitement in your life, but sometimes I think the predictability of it is comforting." She chuckled. "I was talking to Joe's wife the other day, and she said they get into fewer fights now that Edie's cooking for us." In response to George's questioning expression, she added, "He always used to complain when she fixed the same thing for dinner that he had for lunch. Now she knows from day to day what she can't cook."

George smiled. "I suppose you're right. It does simplify things. But maybe we could go out to dinner tonight if the kids don't stop by or—"

The ringing of the telephone cut him off, and Mary, who had sat down at the chair near the desk, stood and answered it. Her eyebrows lifted, and she looked at him. "Just a moment, please," she said. She put her hand over the mouthpiece of the phone and extended it to George. "It's the governor," she whispered.

George felt his stomach give a sickening drop as he took the phone from her.

3

The car began to drift toward the side of the road, and Marian glanced at Stephanie. Her eyes were staring straight ahead, and her hands failed to move on the wheel to correct the drift. Marian frowned.

"*Stephanie*," she said loudly.

Stephanie started, looked at her curiously, and then drew in a sharp breath as she realized what had happened. She turned the wheel back. "I need to stop." She pulled the car onto the shoulder of the road and sat still for a moment.

"What's wrong?"

Stephanie shook her head slightly and felt the veil lift again. As it did so, she took an involuntarily deep breath, and the images came flooding at her. She felt Marian's presence, felt the car running, but these sensations were beginning to fall away.

A sheet of paper appeared at the top of her vision and floated to the left, and to the right, floating down, down. There was a murmur of voices around her, a mingling of odors, and then there was a flash of light playing on metal to her right. She caught a glint out of the corner of her eye, but she felt frozen, her attention on the piece of paper that continued to float down until it left her vision.

Slowly, everything faded, and she was fully in the car again, Marian next to her, a worried look on her face.

"Are you okay?"

Stephanie nodded. And that was when she saw the sign on the shoulder a few yards ahead announcing that the next exit would take them to Hardwick, Georgia.

Marian followed Stephanie's gaze and frowned. "Is there something about that sign, sweetheart?"

Stephanie shook her head. "I don't know. I think so. I saw what I think was the rifle from the nightmare, and there was this piece of paper just floating in the air." She sighed and put the car into forward gear. "I just hope it all clicks into place in time." She watched the traffic flowing north along the interstate and pulled out when there was a break.

4

Later that afternoon, Mary extracted the dark blue suit from her husband's side of the closet and made a soft tsk-tsk sound.

"We've got to get you a new blue suit, honey. This one's not fit to go to a hog callin' in, much less be worn by a state representative." Not getting a response, she turned to George, who was sitting on the side of the bed. He was smiling at her, obviously amused at her unusual fussiness. She put the suit back into the closet and went to stand between his legs and be enfolded in his arms.

"You're being awfully quiet today." She pulled back and smoothed his hair, then ruffled it a bit so that it stuck up in back again.

"I'm just wondering how I'm going to stand being away from you so much. I don't think I'm going to like that at all."

"Well, I know our lives are going to be changed, but it'll only be for three or four months. The legislature rarely lasts past the middle of March. You'll be home on the weekends, and there's no reason why I can't come to Atlanta once a week to see you." She smiled secretively. "And maybe it'll be fun to sleep with you in another bed sometimes."

George grinned, ran his hands down from Mary's waist to her buttocks, and gave her an affectionate squeeze. "I suppose that might be fun. But I have fun with you right here, too." He paused. "You know, you always seem to see the bright side of things. It's kept me going over the years when things were really rough sometimes."

"You made it easy to do."

"Not all the time."

"Well..." She laughed and pushed him backwards on the bed. He grabbed the pockets of her faded blue jeans and pulled her after him so that she rested on top of him. "Mmm. That's nice," she smiled, and then she kissed him lightly. "So, is that why you're so quiet? Thinking about being away from me?"

"That, and I'm wondering why I've been picked to fill Henry's place. "

"Because you're the best person for the job."

"I'm a farmer, Mary. I always have been, and that's all I ever will be."

She chuckled. "You're not exactly a farmer with five acres and a mule, dear. You've worked hard all your life for the people around here. When they tried to put the road through and all of us got upset about it, you got enough people together to make them stop the highway. When the factory closed, you helped the workers get together and find enough money to open another business where they could give their neighbors their jobs back. News gets around when you're a good man."

She moved back a bit and looked at him hard. "What else?"

"I'm worried."

"What about?"

"I like myself the way I am. I've got my faults, but I pretty much like the person I am." He looked at her intently. "What if I get up to Atlanta, and I have to be a politician, and I change? I don't want to start talking out of both sides of my mouth. And I don't want to get so ambitious that I start doing it just to try to get more power."

"You won't. I promise you, if I think you're doing that, I'll jerk you back here so fast you won't know what's happening."

George laughed loudly. "I believe you'd do that."

"You *know* I would."

He turned his head and looked embarrassed. "You know," he said softly, "when I was a kid, my class went through the Capitol. I was awestruck. All those men in those pictures — they were so powerful. The building itself seemed powerful — almost magical. That gold dome. The woman with the torch on top of it." He looked back at her. "The idea that I'm going to be there to make laws for the people of this state is mind-boggling to me."

"Maybe they'll put your picture on one of those walls one day. Maybe as governor."

George groaned and shook his head. "No. No, ma'am. I don't even know if I'd want to stay up in Atlanta longer than the rest of this term. Assuming anybody's even gonna want me to."

"Oh, come on."

"I've got to be realistic, Mary. There are some issues going on that I'd like to have some influence on — some issues that affect the people around here particularly. But I may not be able to do much of anything in the time I'll have before the expiration of Henry's term. It'll only be one session, you know."

"Well, there's the special session this month. You'll get to know your way around so you can jump right in, come January. You'll get something done. Don't worry." She looked at him appraisingly. "You know one thing I like about you?"

George laughed and rolled her over so that he was lying on top. He leaned down and kissed her slowly and felt her move under him. He felt his breath quicken, and he pressed himself forward. "And what is that thing?"

Mary slapped him playfully on the back. "What I meant was that one thing I like about you is that, unlike a lot of men, you let yourself feel—"

George squeezed her hip. "I would say so."

She laughed again and hit him harder. "Stop that. You're just trying to avoid getting a compliment, because you get embarrassed, and you know it. You can feel for other people," she said softly. George's eyes wandered, and she pulled his ears so he looked at her, smiling. "You're a good man, and that's why you were chosen for this job. I'm proud of you. You'll make a good representative. And every once in a while, when I can, I'm going to be right up there in that gallery, watching you."

"Watching me shuffle papers and cough and snore like all the other old men?"

"You don't act like an old man."

"No?" He leaned forward and kissed her slowly. Quite suddenly, he wanted her more than he had wanted her in a long time. The older he got, the less his loins seemed to cooperate with his mind. But now, in the middle of the day, with the sun shining through the lowered blinds, he could feel the strength of his wanting her. He felt her breathing lifting him, and he moved off her just long enough to remove her clothes and then his own, and then he took her with all her little sighings and familiar sounds and smells and warmth and love.

Afterward, when George had gotten up to go to the bathroom, Mary lay there and smiled. It was better than it had been for a while. It was almost always good for her, because George, even when he had trouble taking her in the way he wanted to, made sure she was satisfied. But she liked it this way, too. Hard, and strong, and fast. As if she wouldn't be able to stop him if she wanted to. She smiled again. All it took was a word, and he would stop. Always. But this time, it was as if he wouldn't, and she liked that, too.

She sat up and caught sight of the blue suit in the closet. She hugged her knees. George was going to do a wonderful job. She was going to be prouder of him than she had ever been. And — one of these days, maybe a portrait of him *would* hang in the Capitol among those of the other governors.

She arose, pulled on her jeans and shirt, and turned to tug at the bedspread to straighten it. One of these days, she mused, he just might put Hardwick, Georgia, on the map. She straightened and gave a pillow a final plump. In fact, she thought with a smile, maybe Hardwick would even be a town that would go down in history as the home of a United States president.

PART THREE

1

Corky Edwards's apartment occupied the upper story of a large Victorian house in the Candler Park neighborhood of Atlanta, which young, middle-class professionals had begun moving into and renovating some years earlier. It was a neighborhood where various economic classes, ethnic and racial groups, age groups, and life-styles mixed with relative harmony; where an elderly woman pulling a folding shopping cart down cracked sidewalks lined with huge oak trees might stop to chat with her purple-haired, punk-rocker neighbor; where lesbians and gay men might hold hands with little fear of harassment.

In Corky's three-bedroom apartment, hardwood floors were polished to a sheen, and a huge chandelier, hung from a fourteen-foot ceiling in the dining room, threw gleams of light against the salmon-tinted walls and stark white woodwork. Corky's ability to afford her surroundings, she had assured Stephanie and Marian, were due solely to the fact that she had two roommates who were "uptown dykes," as she put it. Her roommates had assured the two Florida visitors, however, that even though they both worked at prestigious Atlanta law firms, Corky, as a printer, made "more money than the two of us put together."

Because of the mixture of the neighborhood and of the household, where two women set off for work in the morning sporting mandatory business clothes and the third would likely as not have holes in the knees of her jeans, the party itself was attended by a just as seemingly incongruous mixture of people. The majority of party-goers were women, but there were two elderly men, obviously a couple, who lived across the street, and a young man with pink and green streaks in his hair who stayed in the kitchen most of the evening preparing elaborate hors d'oeuvres that were then placed on the table by a black man in his midforties who wore a suit and tie. The music was just as incongruous. An ear-splitting hard-rock selection would be replaced by a soft Meg Christian song, which would be followed by a fifties' oldie.

"I love Corky's parties," Marian said. "However, I find that I have to remember to keep my mouth from falling open sometimes lest I appear rude." She smiled at Stephanie's low chuckle and hooked her arm through Stephanie's. "You remember that first party at Karen's?"

Stephanie frowned slightly and watched as two younger women nearby danced to one of the slower musical selections. "No, I don't believe I do."

Marian lightly punched Stephanie's arm. "You do so, and you know it."

Stephanie grinned and leaned to kiss Marian's cheek. "Of course, I remember. How could I ever forget? As a matter of fact, I was thinking about that just a minute ago."

"Yeah? Really?"

"Really. I was also thinking that I'd like to dance with you."

As Marian smiled and lifted her arms to put them around Stephanie's neck, though, Stephanie's eye was caught by a startlingly bright glint of light that seemed to fill the room for a split second. Afterwards, when it was obvious that no one else had seen the flash, and still holding Marian closely, she swept her gaze across the room. She caught a glimpse of a woman standing near the French doors leading out to the patio, and as she watched, her visioned narrowed, focused. She frowned. It was as if she were staring down a long, dark tunnel, with this woman at the end of it. There were at least three or four women standing near the doors, and yet all she could see was one.

The fear rushed at her again. The room became hazy, and dizziness threatened to overtake her. Without warning, she was back in the warehouse of her nightmare.

The woman was holding a rifle, her eyes bright with insanity, and the crowd was cheering in the terrible street below. As the woman swung the rifle toward the window, Stephanie reached out, her fingertips touching the cold metal of the rifle barrel. The woman turned toward her, and Stephanie saw a tear trickling down her cheek.

"Stephanie? *Stef?*"

Stephanie shook her head and looked around. The room swam back into view, and Marian was standing in front of her, frowning in concern.

"Are you okay?"

Stephanie took a deep breath and released it, then she nodded toward the patio doors. "There was a woman standing over there."

Marian turned to look. "What woman, honey? There are a lot of women."

"I don't know. She was fairly short. I got the impression of a lot of strength — like she might do outdoor work — construction, physical labor of some kind. Short, brown hair."

Marian shrugged. "Well, she's not there now, dear." She looked at Stephanie closely. "What's going on?"

Stephanie brushed her fingers through her hair, trying to shake off the feeling of despair that had settled in the pit of her stomach — a feeling she knew had not arisen from within herself but had come from the woman she had seen. "I think she has something to do with the nightmare."

"We could ask Corky about her. Who she is."

"I suppose." Stephanie grimaced and was silent for a moment, then she sighed. "I don't like the idea of involving anyone else in this, but I don't see any other way to find out what we need to know."

2

Woody stared out the window at the gold dome of the State Capitol, lit up in the night. On top of the dome, although she could not see it because of the distance, she knew there was a woman holding a lighted torch in one hand and a sword in the other. She sneered. The guidebook said the statue represented freedom.

After a moment, she became aware that Helen had entered the room and was talking to her. She turned and saw that Helen was looking worried again. She managed a smile. Helen seemed less worried when she saw a smile.

"Woody?"

"Yeah?"

"It's almost three o'clock. What are you doing?"

"Nothing. Just looking."

"Oh." There was a long pause. "That was a nice party, wasn't it?"

"Mmm." Woody frowned. She was going to have to find out more about the layout of the Capitol, how many guards there were. It startled her when she heard Helen's voice again. She had forgotten Helen was in the room.

"Will you come to bed?"

"In a minute."

Helen nodded and turned. Woody frowned again. Helen looked so sad these days, and she really couldn't understand why. Maybe she would ask her.

She stood, reached to turn off the light beside the window, and caught a glimpse of the gold dome once more. She pulled the chain on the light, and the room fell into darkness. Lowering herself into the window seat again, she stared, mesmerized, at the tiny glint of gold that seemed to hover in the Atlanta skyline.

3

Awakening with a start, it took Marian several seconds to realize that the phone was ringing. She reached over to the nightstand and felt around. Another several seconds and two more rings of the phone passed before she realized that it was not on her side of the bed. She frowned, struggled to a sitting position, and felt disoriented until she remembered they were in the motel. The telephone was on Stephanie's side.

"Stef?" She put a hand on Stephanie's hip and shook her lightly and got only mumbling. The phone kept ringing. Sighing, she crawled over Stephanie's body, trying not to put her knees into any vital areas. She finally reached the phone and lifted the receiver, mercifully stilling the noise. The digital clock on the nightstand clicked over to 3:14 a.m.

"Hello?" she managed. She listened for a moment. "Okay. Let me see if I can wake her up — no, no, that's okay."

She sat on the edge of the bed and shook Stephanie until she saw her eyes open slightly.

"Hmm? What?"

"Close your eyes again. I'm going to turn on the light."

"Mmm. Okay."

Stephanie's eyes closed tightly, and then she made a whining noise as the bedside lamp was switched on. "What is it?"

Marian covered the mouthpiece of the receiver with her hand. "It's Corky."

Stephanie groaned. "Does that woman never sleep?"

"I've often wondered myself. Frankly, I don't think so. She said she figured out just a few minutes ago who you were talking about."

As Stephanie reached for the receiver, Marian said softly, "Be nice, dear. Remember that Corky really is a night person."

Stephanie groaned again and took the receiver.

As Marian listened to Stephanie's half of the conversation, she shivered in the chill of the room and rubbed her bare arms. It took a moment for her to realize that the chill did not come from the temperature of the room.

It occurred to her that she felt afraid.

1

Corky rose slightly from the table and waved a spoon at the short-haired woman behind the counter at the busy neighborhood cafe. She raised her voice in order to be heard above the noise.

"Christ, Nancy, you give me a glass of iced tea that's a foot tall and a stupid spoon that's only six inches long. What do you expect me to do with it?"

The woman turned and shot Corky a significant look across the counter. "In the first place, idiot," the woman called, "you got sweet tea, so you don't need to stir it—"

"But if I put lemon in it, I'm gonna have to—"

"And in the second place, who the hell said you was gettin' lemon? You don't pay enough for food here to get lemon!"

There was laughter from people at other tables, as well as from Stephanie and Marian, and Corky shook her head in mock resignation and sat down. "What can I say? It's true." She smiled, but a moment later, she sobered.

"I don't know what's happened to Woody. I've known her for years, and she's always been a real sweetheart. She'd do anything for you — a hell of a lot more than I'd probably do. Before she and Helen met, she was a little wild. We both did a lot of drinking in our younger days. But after she met Helen, she stopped all that. Oh, she might have a beer now and then with a pizza or a glass of wine at a party, but I've seen her stick to Pepsi all evening, too."

She looked up as Nancy approached and put plates heaped with onion-smothered hamburger steaks, crisp French fries, and coleslaw in front of them. A side dish of green beans obviously seasoned with bacon was placed beside Corky's plate.

Marian groaned. "My cholesterol's going to be sky high."

"I know," Corky said, "but it's worth it. Once in a while, I just have to have real food. Then I can get back to the rabbit stuff and broiled fish."

Stephanie speared a piece of steak generously decorated with grilled onions and rolled her eyes heavenward. "This is wonderful. Do you think we could take her back with us?"

Marian smiled, but her voice held a tinge of gentle sarcasm. "Fine for you, dear. You can eat anything you want, and your cholesterol never goes over one-eighty." She turned back to Corky. "You told Stephanie you keep thinking about something Woody said?"

"Yeah. Something pretty spooky. One night, she and Helen were over playing cards with Sam and me, and Sam — you know how the woman keeps up with the news — well, she started talking about some politician. God knows which one. Take your pick. Anyway, he'd made a ridiculous, asshole statement about how gays shouldn't have children or even be around them because they corrupt the youth of this country, doo-dah, doo-dah. You know the spiel. Well, we all got incensed, of course. I mean, you know that's what most of them think, but when you hear one of them *say* it, it kind of brings up all that anger you walk around with—" She was quiet for a moment and seemed to be concentrating on the green beans, then she looked up at Marian.

"All the pain of not fitting in that you ignore most of the time. Anyway, the only one not saying anything was Woody. When we had sort of run out of things to spout off about, Woody says — very quietly — that maybe we should get rid of people who believe things like that."

Stephanie lifted an eyebrow but said nothing.

Corky caught the look and nodded. "I'm telling you, that's what she said. I mean, we had been saying some pretty violent things, like—" She made her voice deep and gruff. "I think maybe we should string them boys up by the balls." She went back to her natural voice. "But the comments were so extreme as to be ludicrous." She pointed a ketchup-coated French fry at Stephanie. "I'll tell you one thing, Woody's little comment was a pretty effective conversation stopper." She made the French fry disappear in one bite. "Well, we stared at her, and then Helen laughed kind of nervously and said, 'You don't really mean that, of course.' Almost as though she were prompting Woody, you know? So what Woody does is — I mean, it was like Woody was inside of herself, saying what she really, really did think, and then, when it was obvious that we thought she was off the wall, she took stock of the situation and made this one-hundred-and-eighty-degree turn." She tapped the side of her head. "You could almost heard the wheels click. 'I've made a mistake. Better correct it.'"

Marian gave a small shrug. "We all do that from time to time. Depending on how comfortable we feel with a particular opinion, or how much confidence we have in ourselves."

"Yeah, but I got such a weird feeling from it. She just sort of looked up from her cards and glanced around, like she was judging our reaction. And then, all of a sudden, she smiled and gave this little laugh and said, 'I really had you guys going, didn't I?' Well, we just groaned, and to get us off the subject, I started talking about something else. I mean, I sure as fuck didn't want to deal with it, so I copped out. But I'll tell you something, it was spooky."

Corky scooped up coleslaw on her fork and speared a couple of green beans. She chewed for a minute and then pushed the food to one side of her mouth so she could talk. "Actually, if you want to know my personal opinion, I think Woody's snapped." After swallowing, she said, "A couple of times, I've seen her sitting by herself — like at a party or when I've been over to see her and Helen — and she looks like she's listening to somebody. Like somebody's talking to her. And then her lips move, and it looks like she's talking to this other person. Only she's not making any sound." She shook her head. "I hate that. I feel like I ought to be doing something, but what?"

Marian frowned. "Without seeing her, it would be foolish to diagnose it, of course, but it sounds awfully schizophrenic."

Corky grimaced. "That's what I've been thinking."

"Do you think she'll talk to us?" Marian wiped her fingers on the napkin and reached for her iced tea.

"Who? Woody?" A look of disbelief crossed Corky's face. "No way."

"No," Stephanie said. "Helen."

Corky shrugged. "Sure. I don't see why not. We could go over there together, if you want. But be forewarned. When you talk to her, she'll clam up if you mention getting help for Woody. She told me she was after Woody for a while to get help, and Woody got crazy. She disappeared for several days, and Helen got really scared. She's had good years with Woody. Woody's always treated Helen well, and Helen will stick with her till the bitter end. Besides which, I assume Helen can't get her committed without her consent unless Woody actually does something. And if Woody's a schizophrenic, then she's a well-functioning one most of the time." She paused for a moment. "To tell you the truth, I'm not sure Helen could even find it within herself to commit Woody unless Woody did something awfully crazy — violent."

She wadded her napkin, put it over the remains of her meal, and reached for a pack of cigarettes in the breast pocket of her t-shirt. She lit one and leaned back before she spoke again. "But to tell you another truth, I wouldn't be surprised at anything Woody might do any more."

Helen took the last glass of lemonade from the tray on the coffee table and sat back on the sofa. She glanced at Corky, who was lounging in the recliner on the other side of the table, one leg thrown over the arm of the chair.

"Woody felt a tremendous amount of guilt when Katie was taken from us. She thought that if she hadn't been living with us, maybe I wouldn't have lost Katie." She shook her head. "Seeing my pain constantly didn't help, either. I guess it just made things worse." She took a paper napkin from the table and wiped off the moisture that was forming on the glass.

"I assume she felt powerless."

Helen looked toward Stephanie, who had said very little since they had arrived.

"Yes. That was probably the worst."

"Would her parents be able to help at all?" Marian leaned forward and put her glass down on the cork coaster.

Helen laughed, and her voice held more than a tinge of bitterness. "Woody's father found out when his daughter was seventeen that she was queer. Woody doesn't remember that he ever went to church before, but all of a sudden, he 'got religion.' He tried to 'help' her by committing her to a mental institution. A shrink who might have been a little better than most of them there—" She glanced at Marian. "Sorry, but I think the doctors in that particular hospital were unlikely to be worthy of the title of 'doctor.'"

Marian gave her a sympathetic smile. "No apology needed. Unfortunately, there are a lot of bad shrinks out there."

"Anyway," Helen continued, "one of the doctors at the clinic finally met Woody and raised hell because she was there. Rather than going back home, she went to live with her mother's sister in Dallas. A few months later, her older brother, Jerry, got fed up with what was going on at home and moved there, too."

Helen glanced toward Stephanie, who seemed to be avoiding looking at her. "This is a pretty long story. Are you sure you want to hear all of it? It must not be very interesting to—"

Marian turned her gaze toward Stephanie and then back to Helen. "Don't worry about our time. Why don't you just tell us anything that you feel like."

Helen nodded. "Well, when Woody tried to contact her parents later, she learned that her mother had committed suicide a couple of months earlier. Her father had been blaming her mother for his daughter's 'unnatural' condition, and the poor woman couldn't stand up to him any longer. Woody had just turned nineteen. So then he started blaming Woody for her mother's death." She sighed again. "About once a month, she gets a letter from him, all a variation on the theme that she killed her mother and she's gonna burn in hell."

Marian looked down at the glass of lemonade and frowned, then she looked at Helen again. "How about your parents? Would they have any influence with Woody?"

"I haven't seen them in years. They're in Nebraska. My dad's in a nursing home with Alzheimer's disease. My mom has little time to do anything but take care of him, be with him every day. He's probably not going to live very long."

"I'm sorry."

Helen nodded.

"Tell us about the trial," Marian said. "I remember some of it, but what I got was only secondhand, of course."

Helen stared at the glass of lemonade while she talked, her voice quiet. "The trial was horrible. Things were said about Woody and me — and about the way we raised Katie — that were unbelievable. It seemed to drag on forever. They asked Katie questions about whether she had ever seen us in bed, making love. She said she was in bed *between* us when we were doing it." Helen shook her head. "Of course Katie was in bed with us sometimes. Like on a Saturday morning, she'd come in and crawl between us. They'd say, 'Were Woody and your mommy touching each other?' and she'd nod her head. Everybody was trying to be so goddamned careful not to upset her that she didn't know what the hell they were as-king!" Helen stopped for a moment, apparently composing herself, and no one spoke. When she continued, her voice was calmer.

"Afterwards, Doug was given custody of Katie, and I got visitation rights. Once a week, for a few hours, as long as Doug or his parents were with us. It would've been difficult, but we would've managed. Then, two months after the trial, Doug accepted a transfer to Chicago. After that, I guess I lost hope. There was no way, even if I'd been working, to go out there even once a month — twice a year would've been hard — not with the legal fees we'd run up. People were very generous in supporting us, but after a while, we started sending the money back to them. While I wasn't working, we couldn't accept it. It didn't feel right."

Helen took a sip of lemonade and paused. "I stayed out of work for a long time. Months. I couldn't get my job back afterwards, so I started doing word processing as an office temp. While I was out of work, Woody put in extra hours and days at her job — she works for a landscaping service. It was the only thing that kept our heads above water financially. She stayed with me every other waking minute, which was the only thing that kept me going." She looked at Marian. "I really didn't want to live. I'm sure the pain was incredible for Woody, not only because her mother had taken her own life and she was afraid I would do the same thing, but also because of the fact that I still had her, and yet she didn't feel like she was any help. She was, of course. I wouldn't have made it otherwise. But I couldn't convince her of it." She put the glass on the coffee table and rubbed her hands together.

"I found myself wandering from room to room, not knowing half the time where I was, not caring the rest of the time. I'd go past a store window and see a toy and think, 'Katie would like that.' And then I'd remember that even if I sent it to her, I couldn't see her face when she got it." Her voice broke, and she composed herself with a deep breath. "It was like having a wound that wouldn't heal. A wound that the knife twisted in a dozen times a day. Slowly, it's going away." She paused again.

"Not for Woody, though. She wasn't even allowed to talk to Katie after the trial, and she wasn't allowed visitation rights. She didn't let herself grieve like I did, either. She tried to stay strong for me, and she wouldn't allow herself to fall apart like I did. I'm afraid she's fallen apart in another way now." She looked down, and when she looked back up, her voice was shaky. "I'm getting more and more worried about her. She disappears for hours — sometimes for days."

Marian frowned. "Where does she go? Does she say?"

Helen shook her head. "No. I've tried to get her to tell me, but she just gets angry. Frankly, I'm not sure she knows herself. One day, her boss called me at work. He said she hadn't been in for three days, and he wanted to know if she was sick." She looked at Marian, and her voice was soft, intense. "But every day that week, she'd been coming home exhausted, her clothes dirty like she'd been at work. I asked her how work was, and she told me stuff that had happened during the day — what somebody said, where they'd been working. I still haven't figured it out." She took a deep breath and sighed. "She must've gone back to work, though, because she's been bringing home a paycheck." She hesitated for a moment, then looked at Stephanie. "Corky says you can get into people's minds or something."

"I'm a psychic counselor. At times, I can enter a person's consciousness."

"Do you think you can help us? I don't have much money."

Stephanie shook her head. "Money's not an issue, Helen. I'm just not sure that what I have to do is anything that's going to help you."

Helen frowned. "I don't understand. What you have to do?"

Stephanie rubbed at her eyes and stood up. She wandered toward the casement window on the other side of the living room, feeling drawn there, but she became distracted when Helen asked her another question.

Suddenly, without warning, she saw sunlight glinting off a rifle barrel. It seemed to move toward the window, and the fear that welled up in her chest constricted her breathing. After what seemed like an eternity, as if from a long way off, she heard Marian's voice.

"Are you all right, sweetheart?"

Stephanie shook her head and smiled with difficulty. "Yes. I'm fine."

"I don't understand what's going on," Helen said.

Stephanie brushed her fingers through her hair and took a deep breath. "What I'm saying is that I'd like to help you and Woody. I'm just not sure what I have to do is going to help Woody."

Helen looked agitated now. "You keep saying 'What I have to do.' What is that?"

"I'm not sure yet."

"I'm sorry," Helen said, "but I just don't understand."

"Look," Marian said, "sometimes Stephanie gets impressions about something that's going to happen in the future. Something she has to — do something about." She shrugged helplessly. "It's hard to explain. But in this particular case, apparently Woody is involved in whatever's going on."

"Woody's involved? In what?"

Marian started to speak, but Stephanie stopped her. "Helen," she said quietly, "I have reason to believe that Woody is going to try to kill someone."

Helen gave an abrupt, disbelieving laugh. "That's ridiculous. Woody couldn't hurt a fly. She would never try to hurt someone."

Corky had been quiet, but she spoke now, her voice intense. "Woody's changed a lot, Helen. You know it, and I know it. You've got to stop kidding yourself about just how much she's changed. You see her every day, so maybe it's harder for you to see. She's capable of something now that she didn't used to be capable of."

Helen's body stiffened noticeably. "I don't know what you mean."

"She *has* changed, *hasn't* she?"

It was Stephanie who had spoken, and Marian glanced at her in surprise at the sharp tone of her voice.

"Well, she's quieter," Helen said softly.

"And she's been doing strange things lately?"

Marian saw tears come to Helen's eyes, and she considered that perhaps Helen had been pushed far enough. "Stephanie," she started, "maybe—"

Stephanie shook her head. "No, Marian. It's not right to tell her we're going to help her. We probably won't. Can't. It's necessary for her to know." She turned to Helen. "Woody's planning to kill someone. I don't know who yet, and I don't know when. But I know she's planning to do it. And I need your help."

Helen laughed shortly. "Help you stop Woody from killing somebody? First of all, Woody couldn't kill anybody. I told you that. And second, you talk about helping us, and then in the next breath, you say maybe you won't be helping us. Or can't. I don't see that it makes much difference which it is. Well, you don't have to help us, but I'm not going to listen to any more of this about Woody." She stood up. "I'm sorry, but I want you to leave."

Marian spoke soothingly. "Please, Helen. You've got to realize that we do want to help. It's just that we don't know enough yet about what's going on." She looked at Stephanie, hoping that perhaps Stephanie had reconsidered her stern attitude and would soften enough to smooth things over in time to persuade Helen to continue talking to them. Stephanie, however, was looking out the window again, and her back was as stiff as Helen's, unyielding.

"I want you to leave," Helen said abruptly. "Woody and I are doing fine. She's not going to hurt anybody. Would you leave, please?"

"Helen," Corky said, "I'm sure you remember that time over at my place when Woody said she thought it would be a good idea to get rid of people who thought that gays shouldn't be around children."

"She was just kidding about that, Corky. You should know that—"

"Bullshit," Corky said softly.

"Corky—" Helen's voice held a note of pleading.

"And don't look at me like you think I'm some kind of goddamned traitor. I love you, and I love Woody, and I'm scared for her. She's not really herself any more. I think you need to get your head out of the sand."

"Don't tell me what you think I need. Woody and I have been doing just fine."

"Bullshit again," Corky said.

The two stared at each other for a long time, and finally, Helen gave a small cry and threw the napkins she had been holding down on the table.

"Oh, damn." She looked back at Corky, her eyes flooding with tears, and Corky went to sit by her and rock her through the brief storm, soothing her, stroking her back and hair, letting her cry.

After the storm had passed, Helen looked up and said softly, "God, I've been so scared."

3

Marian watched as Stephanie stood in the small alcove outside the motel bathroom and undressed. As each item of clothing was removed, it was folded neatly and draped over the back of the nearby chair. Stephanie's despondency, Marian thought, was evident even in her movements. It was all well and good for Stephanie to possess a talent that could help someone, but when Stephanie knew that someone would be hurt, it was a different story. And obviously she believed that Helen was going to be hurt, even after everything the young woman had already gone through. It was no wonder that Stephanie felt that her psychic ability was more a cage than anything else.

"I really thought when Helen broke down that she was going to let us do something to help," Marian said.

Stephanie looked up. "I know you did. I keep telling you, I'm not sure we can." Without waiting for a reply from Marian, she went into the bathroom and closed the door.

Moments later, while Stephanie was still in the shower, the phone rang. Marian picked it up, spoke for a few minutes, and then, with a frown, hung up the receiver.

Stephanie came through the bathroom door, toweling her hair. "Helen?"

"Mmm. She says she's sorry she got so upset. Apparently, when Woody got home this evening, everything was fine. She's smiling, affectionate, etcetera, etcetera."

"And she didn't want to talk to me."

"No."

Stephanie turned and draped the damp towel over the rack beside the sink in the alcove. "On some level, she knows everything's not fine, but she wants to believe it so much, she's ignoring what's really going on. She was afraid that if she talked to me, I'd convince her otherwise."

"I think you're right." Marian paused. "You know, she said Woody is so calm now. It reminded me of how people sometimes get very calm when they decide they're going to commit suicide. You think anything like that's going on?"

"Not suicide, but the behavior is similar to what you're talking about. She's been in a confused state — in the middle of a war between her natural impulse toward peace and her disturbed impulse toward violence. Much like the conflict a potential suicide experiences before the decision is made. The calm she feels now stems from the fact that she's made up her mind what she's going to do, even though she doesn't have a plan yet. She's not confused any more. At least not about what she thinks she needs to do. Before, she was just dangerous to herself. Now, she's dangerous to somebody else."

"Makes sense. But you don't know yet who she's dangerous to, right?"

Stephanie found a comb beside the sink and began pulling it through her hair. "No. And I think it's going to be a while before I do. All we can do is go back home and wait."

Marian studied Stephanie carefully. "Why were you so abrupt with Helen this afternoon? It isn't like you."

Stephanie shrugged, but she avoided Marian's gaze. "I'm anxious about this. That's all."

"Yeah, right." She watched as Stephanie glanced up in the mirror over the sink to look at her. "Look," Marian said, "don't give me that. I have no doubt at all that you're anxious about something, but it's not what you're saying it is."

"It's not enough that this woman is running around thinking of killing someone?"

"It's been my experience, dear, that people get politicized out of their emotions. Their emotions are what motivate them to do something they already believe they should do. But something has to affect them personally, then they can carry it outward to society." She saw Stephanie open her mouth, and she held her hand up.

"For example, maybe you know that disabled people have a hard time getting around in the world because of all of the physical barriers that exist, and you might even do a little to help in that struggle. But then, maybe one day your lover has a stroke or she's in an automobile accident, and she's left paralyzed for a period of time, maybe even the rest of her life, and you suddenly realize just how heartbreaking those barriers can be. It touches you personally now."

Stephanie had been leaning on the edge of the counter, looking down, but her head came up now, and Marian saw her staring into the mirror at her.

"I've struck a nerve, haven't I?"

Stephanie turned and leaned back against the counter. "Maybe. "

"So — what is it?"

Stephanie shook her head slightly.

"Don't do this," Marian said quietly. "I mean it. Whatever's going on, I'm involved in it, if for no other reason than that we're together. Am I involved in any other way?"

Stephanie sighed and went to sit on the bed. She reached over to the nightstand and got a cigarette. When she had it lit, she turned to Marian. "I'm not sure. A couple of nights ago, after you had gone to bed, I was sitting in the living room for a while, finishing a book I'd been reading earlier. When I got up to go to bed, I went to turn off the porch light, and I suddenly started thinking about the child you're going to have."

"The child *we're* going to have?"

"The child *we're* going to have." Stephanie took Marian's hand and looked at it, avoiding Marian's eyes. "All of a sudden, I saw an image of him. Maybe about three years old or so." In response to a question Marian was about to ask, Stephanie said, "Yes. I knew it was him. Not just what he looked like, but an unmistakable 'knowing' that it was him." She looked up. "Do you know what I mean?"

Marian nodded. "As much as I'm able to." She felt a sudden drop of her stomach, and she found that she unconsciously had put her hand on her midsection.

"He was standing there, smiling at me, and there was a man kneeling beside him, with his arm around the boy's shoulders. It seemed to be a protective gesture."

Marian frowned. "Who was it?"

Stephanie shook her head. "I don't know." She held Marian's eyes for a moment. "I do know that it's the man that Woody is a threat to." She leaned over and flicked an ash into the ashtray, and her voice grew even quieter. "I have a strange feeling that the man may be the president one day."

Marian stared at Stephanie and said nothing for a long minute, then she laughed abruptly. "Of the United States?"

"Yes."

Marian laughed again, but her voice held no mirth. "And our son is going to know him?"

"I think so."

"Then doesn't that say that whomever Woody is gunning for is not going to die?"

"Not necessarily."

"Why the hell not? It would seem to me that if you see him with our son three years from now, obviously he has to be alive."

Stephanie said nothing, and a look of concern crossed Marian's face. "Well, what else do you think it could mean?"

"It could mean that he'll know this man *if* this man lives."

"And if this man doesn't live?"

Stephanie shrugged. "I don't know. It may be that he's very important to the boy's future and that if he doesn't live, then the boy's future will be considerably different." She took a deep breath and released it slowly. "I do believe that their lives are somehow intertwined." She leaned over and put out the cigarette. "You were right about how people get involved, though. I was considering letting this one go. Trying to let it go. And then this came at me. Hard."

"How soon is all of this going to happen? Do you know?"

Stephanie shook her head. "It'll be a while, I think."

"Then there's no point in worrying about it right now," Marian said, but her tone failed to match her words. She tugged gently at Stephanie, and Stephanie lay down beside her. They were silent for a while, holding one another closely, before Marian spoke.

"If you could make contact with Woody, you could get into her head and tell what she's planning." She sighed. "But you won't do that, right?"

"Right. I won't do it without her permission."

The barest hint of a smile appeared on Marian's mouth. "You'll only do it with lovers?"

"Only with you. And you gave your permission a long time ago."

"I suppose I did," Marian whispered, "but you could at least be gracious enough not to remind me."

Stephanie smiled, but after a moment, the smile disappeared quietly. "You know," she said, "I was thinking just before the phone rang, what would I do if what happened to Woody and Helen happened to us?" She paused. "Do you ever think about Talbot?"

Marian's brow knitted in thought. "Sometimes. But then I think about the baby, and I tell myself that it's going to be yours and mine. And I try to remember that Frank Talbot — as psychotic as he was — maybe couldn't have done anything other than what he did, and that maybe — if there is a plan to all this — that it couldn't have happened any other way. I don't know if that's true. But I'd rather believe that than think about the fear and the anger. I'd rather believe that there was some reason behind it."

She tapped Stephanie's arm. "You know, I read once — I don't remember where, and I'm not sure I'm quoting accurately — that if God made the earth in seven days, at least allegorically speaking, and that She — I am sure that the writer didn't say She — but if She made the world perfect, then maybe this is Friday afternoon. It's just not finished yet. What do you think?"

"I don't know. For the time being, I guess I believe that we find meaning in what happens to us or we go insane, or we live out our lives unhappy — discontented. If we're able to find the good in what happens, then we live more fully. If we can't, then—"

Marian touched the scar on Stephanie's face. "Like your sister?"

"Like my sister. I can't find any good in what happened that day."

They lay quietly again. After a while, Marian turned on her side, and Stephanie curled up behind her back, her arms around Marian. She caressed the silky, warm skin of Marian's belly with her fingertips. Moments passed, and then she mumbled against the side of Marian's neck, "What're you thinking?"

There was a short silence, and Marian laughed softly, her stomach moving convulsively under Stephanie's hand.

Stephanie raised her head. "Are you laughing at me?"

Marian nodded.

Stephanie smiled, although she wasn't sure what she was smiling about. She turned Marian over, and Marian allowed her laughter to become a chuckle. Then, still smiling, she touched Stephanie's cheek.

"I just think sometimes that it's funny that you ask me what I'm thinking about when it's so easy for you to know."

A grin spreading across her face, Stephanie said, "Would you want me to know all the time?" Marian gave a fake groan. "God, no." Stephanie lifted an eyebrow. "You mean there are things you would prefer I not know you're thinking? That makes me curious."

Marian gave her a mock-innocent look. "Why, nothing, dear. I just wouldn't want you to strain yourself, that's all."

"Uh-huh."

Marian smiled and sighed and snuggled into the crook of Stephanie's arm. "You know, I appreciate your restraint, but there are times when I wish your ethical considerations weren't so strong." There was a silence. "I guess."

"You mean like with Woody."

"Yep." Marian traced a finger from the middle of Stephanie's chest to her navel and grinned when Stephanie shivered.

"That tickles."

"I know. Why do you think I did it?"

Stephanie grabbed Marian's hand and held it still. "It's the age-old question, isn't it?"

"Which age-old question is that?"

Stephanie reached out her right hand, picked up another cigarette and her lighter, and manipulated them both until she had a lit cigarette. She set the ashtray on her stomach, then watched as the curtains fluttered in the slight breeze coming in the window.

"The 'does-the-end-justify-the-means' age-old question."

"Oh. That one."

"Mmm. Or it could be another age-old question."

"There's more than one?"

"Always."

"And which is this one?" Marian struggled feebly to free her hand, and Stephanie finally brought the hand to her mouth, kissed the back of it, and let it go, where it drifted to the inside of her thigh.

"Well, perhaps the one about whether the rights of a few should be sacrificed for the benefit of the many."

"Always a toughie." Marian nodded her head sagely.

"Are you not in the mood for a serious discussion?"

Marian sighed. "Actually, what I was doing was trying to push it away. It keeps coming up though, doesn't it?"

"We don't have to talk about it now."

Marian sighed and patted Stephanie's thigh, then she sat up and brushed her fingers through her hair. She drew her knees up and rested her arms on them and her chin on her arms.

"It'll just keep coming up again."

"Marian," Stephanie said softly, "even if I were to tell somebody about this, what difference would it make? They'd want proof of it. Something Woody said that was a direct threat, something she did. She's said or done nothing so far that could in the least be considered criminal." She laughed shortly. "Can you see it now? 'Officer, you see there's this woman who wants to kill the governor of Texas. Or maybe it's the governor of Georgia. Maybe. Or would you know by any chance if the president is passing through this way any time soon?' And he would say—"

"Or she," Marian mumbled against her arms.

"Or she. And she or he would say, 'How do you know this?' And I'd say, 'Oh, I just jumped into her mind one day and saw it happening, and besides that, I've been having these perfectly hideous nightmares about John Kennedy being murdered, and—'" She gave Marian a significant look, ground out the cigarette in the ashtray, and moved the ashtray back to the nightstand.

Marian studied Stephanie out of the one eye that was visible at the crook of her elbow. "We could get somebody else to call them."

"Like who?"

"Like maybe Dempsey. He could lend credibility. I mean, he's been a sheriff for a long time now. I suspect he's got a great many contacts."

Stephanie studied her for a moment and then closed her eyes. "Don't you think they would want to know how the sheriff of a small Georgia county would know that? They would want to pick up the person who told him, they would want to have proof, etcetera, etcetera, etcetera."

"We could think of some way to do it. To make it plausible."

"Well, even if we could, that leads us back to the other question."

Marian sighed. "Do you have the right to enter her mind to find out what she's planning to do and when."

"Exactly."

"Perhaps one could argue that the wrong of invasion of privacy weighs less than the right of saving the life of a man who might be important to this country." Marian bit at her lip briefly. "I dislike the way that sounds. There have been too many dictators who thought they had the right to take away individual freedoms to save the state." She took a deep breath and released it. "And now, of course, I have an even greater stake in it, don't I?"

"Maybe not," Stephanie said softly. "Maybe I'm wrong about the boy."

Marian shook her head slowly. "No," she whispered. "I don't think so. I've got this feeling in the pit of my stomach that says you're right."

Stephanie stretched out her arm and waited as Marian moved to lie beside her. They both lay staring up at the ceiling for a long time, but even after Marian drifted into a fitful sleep, Stephanie could not join her in that temporary release from the fear that had clouded the last few days for her. She had not told Marian everything. And she was not sure she could, because she was not sure she could accept it herself.

1

"I need a rifle."

"Who doesn't these days?" The man behind the counter, in his midthirties, sported an obviously new military-style haircut that had left a strip of white skin between the hairline and the sun-browned skin on his neck.

"Everybody?" Woody glanced up from the handguns in the glass display case.

"Nowadays, you got to protect yourself." He placed his hands on the counter, stiffened his elbows, and leaned toward her. "There's a lot of weirdos running around out there. You know what I mean?" He gave her a look that apparently was meant to convey some bit of information that his words had not.

Woody stared at him hard, and he relaxed his elbows, took a step backwards, and folded his arms across his chest. He coughed slightly.

"So what do you think you want?"

"I need something with a range of about—" She looked around. "It has to be accurate from about here to," she pointed to the parking lot, "that blue Chevy out there." She frowned. That seemed to be about the right distance, she thought, but it was difficult to tell.

The salesman continued to look at her, and then he laughed, almost a nervous sound. "You need it to be accurate from here to," he pointed, "there."

"Yeah." Woody had looked down into the display case again, but she lifted her head and stared at him flatly. "Is that a problem?"

"No." He barked out the nervous laugh again. "It just sounds pretty funny."

"Funny?"

"Well, most people ask for a range of fifty yards, a hundred yards, something like that. You sound like you've got a particular target in mind."

Woody continued to stare at him. Something was wrong again. Like when she was talking to that woman at the Capitol. She had said too much in some way. She forced a smile.

"Well, you know, I don't know how far that is. A friend and I go out to Pickens County sometimes and shoot at some bottles we line up in front of a bank out in the woods. It looks about that far." She kept her gaze on him. "Do you have anything like that, or not?"

The clerk moved forward again, a slight smile trying to make itself known on his face. "Oh, we got all kinds." He turned, slid the glass door open on the wall display case behind him, and pulled out a long-barreled rifle. He placed it on the countertop with just enough care to avoid breaking the glass. Then he pulled out two more and lined them up.

"Now right here, we've got—" He picked up the first one.

Woody frowned at the huge, long-barreled rifle. "That one's too big. Tell me about this one." She pointed to the last one he had taken out.

The salesclerk shrugged and picked it up. "Well, it's got a range of—" He grinned. "It'll shoot from here to there and a whole lot farther." When he got no response from his customer, the smile slipped from his face.

"What will it do?"

"What do you mean?"

Woody looked at him. "What will it do to the target?"

"Well, it'll sure blow a bottle to hell and back." He laughed until he saw that Woody was staring at him without any show of amusement. The laugh died abruptly, and he coughed again to cover it up.

"And what if I need it for — protection?"

The salesclerk looked hard at her for a minute. "Lady," he said softly, "this mother is gonna blow a man's head off if he's any closer to you than fifty yards. At a hundred yards, it's gonna make a big hole, and there's gonna be more blood than you're gonna want to think about." He nodded to the other two. "Any of these'll do that." He turned and reached into a drawer in back of him. Turning back around, he placed a box on the counter. "And with these hollow-point shells, even with a handgun, there's gonna be a hole big enough to drive a truck through when it comes out."

"Hollow point?"

"They explode on impact. They don't even let cops in some cities use 'em. They had a big row in Atlanta a while back about 'em. They got more stopping power than you'll ever need unless you're hunting elephants—" He grinned again. "And you ain't hunting elephants, are you, little lady?" When he saw Woody staring at him, he looked back down at the box of shells. "They enter a man's body, explode, and make a bigger hole coming out than they when went in. His guts — or brains — are lying all over the place. Believe me, the bastard's dead."

Woody continued to study him for a moment, then she reached into her back pocket, pulled out her wallet, and nodded at the rifle. "How much is it?"

He pushed the rifle across the counter.

Woody looked at it hard, and then the voice down there was saying something to her. It was faint. She cocked her head to the side and listened, and then she frowned. Indeed, how was she going to carry it?

"Will it come apart?"

"What?" The man looked puzzled.

"I need to carry it in two pieces." She looked up, and he had a strange look on his face.

When he saw her staring at him, he swallowed with seeming difficulty and turned back to the case.

"I think I've got something right here you can use," he said quietly.

2

Helen straightened the papers on her desk and swiveled around to face the word processor again. She stared at it for long minutes before she realized what she was doing. Nothing. Again, she thought, she was doing nothing. If she didn't watch it, she was going to be without a job, too.

She pushed the chair back and went to the break room and got a Coke. Sitting at the small table, she put her head in her hands for a moment and then leaned back in the chair with a sigh. She knew *she* had been doing nothing. What she had been trying not to think about was what *Woody* could be doing.

Woody's boss had called her this morning just as she had been leaving the apartment to tell her that if Woody didn't show up today, she was going to be canned. She had been puzzled. "What do you mean if she doesn't show up today?" she had asked. "You sound as if she hasn't been coming in to work again." And that's exactly what he meant, he had said.

Everything was getting worse, she thought. Their lives seemed to be falling apart around them. She had considered calling Stephanie and Marian again, but every time she reached for the phone, she couldn't go through with it. They wanted Woody sent away. And she didn't think Woody would let that happen. Woody would probably kill herself first.

But was Woody really planning to kill someone else? She took a sip of the Coke. It was just so hard to believe. Woody was always so affectionate, so helping and generous with almost everyone. Or at least she had been. Lately, it was hard to be in the same room with her. She just didn't seem to be there.

And then yesterday, she had seemed like her old self again.

Woody had popped out of bed early and almost dragged Helen, laughing delightedly at Woody's exuberant mood, out of bed after her. They had stopped by a Po' Folks restaurant for a fried-chicken picnic lunch and driven out to Stone Mountain Park for the day.

It had been wonderful, Helen mused, just like when they first met. Woody was sweet, romantic. They sat on a blanket with their lunch and looked up at the carving of the generals on the face of the mountain and then took the tram car to the top of "the largest granite outcropping in the world," Woody kept saying. From there, they looked out over what seemed to be half the state of Georgia, their arms around each other, ignoring the sidelong glances from those around them. Helen smiled, remembering. Woody had been laughing, joking like in the past.

Then, this morning, she had found Woody sitting in the window seat, staring out the window, her lips moving as if she were talking to someone. Woody was gone from her again.

She pressed the heels of her hands against her eyes in an attempt to stop the stinging tears. She was tired of crying, tired of worrying about what to do. She pulled a Kleenex out of the pocket of her skirt and blew her nose, then she took a deep breath, squared her shoulders, and stood up.

She wasn't going to let herself fall apart. Woody needed her, and she was going to be there for Woody. They had spent too many good years together for her to let them go now. Woody had been strong for her once. Now she had to be strong for Woody. She would stand by her, no matter what happened.

Helen felt a sob rise in her throat again, and she pushed it back down, willed herself to hold her head up.

No matter what happened.

PART
FOUR

WEDNESDAY

4

OCTOBER

1989

1

"Please sit down, Darryl."

"Okaaay."

Ellen Cheatham managed a small smile as her pupil took a seat in the House of Representatives gallery, and she wondered again if this had been such a good idea. Taking thirty-two squirming children on a field trip had never been her idea of fun, even with a couple of mothers to assist her. But at least the legislature was not in session. Watching as her two mothers took seats with the children, she decided to stand in back of the last row of seats so she could supervise from a better vantage point.

She heard voices behind her and turned slightly to look at the gallery door. A young woman holding what looked like a case for a musical instrument was standing at the door talking to the guard. She lifted an eyebrow. Wouldn't it be strange, she considered, if someone could carry something like that and bring a bomb in? She laughed at herself. She was going to have to stop reading so many spy thrillers. Even so, she was glad the guards were diligent.

A shrill shriek pierced her thoughts, and she turned back to see Darryl yanking Melinda's hair. Shaking her head, she went to play referee again.

2

"Sorry, but I've got to look every time."

"That's okay. It's your job."

Woody bent and opened the black leather case she was carrying. As she popped the metal latches, the guard took a perfunctory glance into the case, in which rested two pieces of a trombone. The guard grunted, and Woody closed the case again.

"You got a music lesson before you come here or something?"

"Yeah."

"You go to Georgia State?"

Woody was already looking into the gallery. A group of children was sitting in the front three rows. She frowned. After a moment, she realized the guard was still speaking to her.

"What?" She looked toward the children again.

"I said, when I was a kid, my old lady made me take up the violin for a while. Luckily, it got to be too expensive. How long you been playing that thing?"

Woody was suddenly aware of a silence, and she looked at the guard. Had he said something? She had to concentrate even harder now in order to follow what was going on around her. It was as if she were wandering around in a jungle of constantly tangled thoughts. And it was getting harder to distinguish the voice inside of her from the voices outside.

The worst part, though, was that she was never sure any more where her own voice was.

"The nightmares are getting even worse, aren't they?"

Marian stood and watched the lights on the yacht in Matanzas Bay twinkle across the black water. A few seconds later, the wake of the yacht reached the Bridge of Lions, and the water slapped around the sea-weathered pilings below them. She turned and looked at Stephanie. A breeze caught her hair and brushed it gently across her face, and she pushed it back.

"Yes. They seem to be intruding on waking hours now."

Marian frowned. "That sounds serious." She was silent for a moment, and then she said quietly, "You know, dear, perhaps you don't have to involve yourself in this."

Stephanie turned to look at her. "Really? And what about the boy?"

Marian closed her eyes briefly. When she opened them, she avoided Stephanie's gaze. What caught her attention for a moment were the kids playing at the city's miniature-golf course across the street from the plaza where the Old Market stood. "Maybe you're being told this man is going to live and that he's going to help us. Maybe that's all it is."

"Maybe." Stephanie turned back to gaze out over the railing into the dark water. The psychic curtain she drew about herself had been seeming more and more like a prison in recent days. It was becoming harder to reach out through the bars to touch even Marian — to allow Marian to touch her. All she wanted to do was retreat inside herself. Marian broke into her thoughts.

"I hate to see you tearing yourself apart."

"Maybe it's our destiny." Stephanie avoided looking at her.

Marian smiled slightly. "Destiny? I seem to recall having had this conversation before, friend."

Stephanie shrugged and said nothing.

"What are you finding so hard to talk about?" Marian leaned closer and touched Stephanie's hand gently.

Normally, when Stephanie's wall went up, Marian let it be, knowing that in a matter of hours or sometimes even days,

Stephanie would come to grips with whatever she was avoiding. But once in a while, Marian would feel that it was time for her to push against the wall that Stephanie had erected — to push just hard enough to create the pressure Stephanie needed to break through to the other side.

"Don't shut me out, sweetheart," she said softly.

Stephanie reached into the pocket of her light windbreaker and took out a pack of cigarettes. She shook a cigarette out and waited until she had it lit before she spoke.

"You know, when Kennedy was killed, I didn't know anything about it. I was as shocked as anyone. Friends who knew about my—" she hesitated, "my ability, kept asking me why I hadn't known it was going to happen. After all, a lot of psychics came forward to say they had warned the White House — or tried to — weeks before it happened. I didn't know why I hadn't 'gotten the message,' so to speak. At some point, I realized that it was because it wasn't for me to know — wasn't for me to do anything about."

There was a moment of silence before Marian spoke again. "This is hard to say," she started, "but perhaps it wasn't for *anyone* to do something about. Perhaps it was supposed to happen that way."

"Do you really believe that?" Stephanie frowned in the darkness.

"Not in my practical, everyday, walking-around self. But on some level, on a much higher level perhaps, I wonder if we don't all choose when we die. Maybe he had done what he could. Maybe it was time."

Stephanie turned and looked at Marian steadily. "Well, this time," she said softly, "it *is* for me to know — to do something about. And I get the distinct impression that I'm the only one who knows about it."

"It sounds to me as if you're saying that you have somehow been — chosen."

Stephanie looked away. "I don't like that word. It sounds too egotistical. Too powerful. I don't want that kind of power. It's too much."

"No," Marian said gently. "No one should have to carry that kind of burden." She took Stephanie's hand and held it. "What if the same thing happens this time? What if no one's in danger except this one man you keep seeing? And what if you can't prevent his death?"

"I just don't know." Stephanie sighed and turned to lean against the iron railing. The lights glowed around Fort Matanzas across the water and spotlighted the palms rising around the 200-year-old fort. The palms along Matanzas Boulevard waved in the breeze that was picking up. Stephanie continued to look out at the bay. She was silent for a long time, and Marian did not break the silence. Finally, Stephanie said, "So you really think there's such a thing as destiny?"

"I think it's possible."

A flicker of a smile appeared at the corner of Stephanie's mouth. "Even in your practical, everyday, walking-around self?"

Marian arched a eyebrow. "I concede nothing."

Stephanie chuckled and put her arm around Marian's waist. "Nothing?"

"Nothing without a struggle."

"That sounds interesting."

"It does, doesn't it?"

"Mmm." She took Marian's elbow and began guiding her toward one of the stone guard towers that protruded from the side of the bridge.

"Where are we going?"

They rounded the tower, and Stephanie came to a stop at the apex of the semicircle of railing. She took Marian in her arms, out of sight of the traffic that flowed over the bridge.

"And just what," Marian said with a smile, "do you think you're doing?"

"This," Stephanie said, and she leaned forward and kissed Marian firmly, sensuously, lingering a long time, teasing at her lips, feeling Marian melt in her arms. When she finally pulled back, Marian's eyes were slightly glazed.

"Mmm. Right out here in front of God and everybody?"

"Nobody can see us."

"Unless somebody comes walking over the bridge."

Stephanie backed her against the rough stone of the tower, farther out of sight, and pulled her close again. Kissing Marian even longer this time, she ran her hands down to the full hips and squeezed firmly.

Marian moaned softly. "Sweetheart," she whispered, "if you keep this up, you're going to have trouble on your hands."

"It doesn't feel like trouble," Stephanie murmured. Her hands moved lower, and she began sliding them up Marian's skirt.

Marian giggled. "Quit that! Somebody really could see us." She hugged Stephanie hard. "If it were just a little more private, I'd make love with you right here. But I'm afraid it's just too public for me to be able to let go the way I want to. Okay?" She touched Stephanie's cheek lightly.

Stephanie groaned in mock pain and then smiled. "Okay, you're right."

Minutes later, they were in the car on their way home when Stephanie pulled off on a side street.

"Where are we going now? I thought you were in a rush to get me home and into bed, dear."

"I'm in a rush to make love to you." Stephanie wiggled her eyebrows comically, and at the next corner, she took a right and ended up on a street that Marian recognized.

"Gary and Jenny's house is down here."

"Mmm."

Marian grinned. "What in God's name are you doing?"

"You'll see," Stephanie said. She drove to the end of the street and pulled into the last driveway on the left. The drive curved around behind the house, where huge trees in back and on both sides of the house hid the backyard from view. It was dark; the only illumination came from the lights lining the sidewalk to the patio. She cut the engine and turned to Marian, who was shaking her head in apparent disbelief.

"You're kidding, right?"

Stephanie got out of the car and went around to Marian's side. She opened the door and held out her hand. "Gary and Jenny went down to the Keys for a week. Didn't they say something about that at dinner the other night?"

"Now that you mention it, I do believe they did." She raised an eyebrow. "And what's that got to do with you and me, friend?"

Stephanie smiled, took Marian's hand, and waited until she got out of the car. Opening the back door, she waved Marian, who was looking at her in disbelief, into the backseat and followed her in.

"Now what?" Marian queried, her face almost hidden in deep shadows.

"Now this," Stephanie murmured in response.

Taking Marian's face in her hands, she leaned forward, placed her mouth on Marian's, and felt Marian's lips part beneath hers. She kissed her deeply and lovingly and long, and when she drew back, Marian's eyes were still closed.

"Oh, that," Marian whispered.

Stephanie smiled and leaned forward once more and felt Marian's arms go around her neck to pull her close. She held onto Marian tightly for long moments, savoring the warm, familiar fragrance of Marian's body, the sensuality of heated, silky skin beneath her hands, the small, murmuring breaths against her ear.

And as she gave herself to the loving embrace, she felt the crystal-like bars of her cage shatter harmlessly and fall away in a soul-sighing release.

Ezrah Palmer looked down the long hallway and frowned. Striding toward the gallery door, about halfway down the hallway in front of him, was a young woman with a black leather case. There was something familiar about her. Or something he was supposed to remember. After a moment, though, when he couldn't get a handle on it, he shrugged and turned to go back to the guard room.

In the middle of the turn, it popped out of his memory like a snake darting out of its hole. *It was the woman his mother had told him about.* He faced down the hallway again and felt his stomach give a little jump. The case she was carrying. There was something about the case. Or the way she was carrying it.

He began to walk faster. He saw Charles Becker smiling at her, talking to her as if they were old friends. The guard looked up and saw him coming toward them, and then the woman was putting the case down on the floor, flipping the latches.

His heart beating faster, he began to trot down the hall toward them. As he came to a halt in front of them, he realized his hand had automatically gone to the butt of his pistol in its holster.

Becker glanced up, a puzzled look on his face, then he looked down at the case. When his eyes met Ezrah's again, the look on his face had changed to one of derision. Dismayed, Ezrah realized that Becker knew what he had been thinking and that he had been wrong.

With a nonchalant flip of his wrist, Becker flipped the lid of the case open to reveal a trombone. He looked back up at Ezrah.

"A trombone, Ezrah," Becker said.

He might as well have said "nigger" instead of "Ezrah"; that was the word that was in his eyes. It was something Charles Becker had called him before. Not to his face, of course, but he had heard him spouting off in the guard room one day as he was about to enter. And he could hear the story that would be told now. "That nigger thought that little girl was carrying a bomb in there or something. Scared the shit out of him." And then the contemptuous laughter.

"She carries it all the time."

"What?" Ezrah looked up from the trombone.

"I *said*, 'She carries it all the time.'"

"Oh," Ezrah mumbled. He saw the woman staring at him intently, a strange look in her eyes — not quite a look of fear, but more as if she were on the edge and was wondering which way she was going to fall. He could see why his mother had thought something was wrong.

Becker latched the case, picked it up, and handed it to her with a courteous near-flourish, touching the brim of his cap with his fingertips in a half salute. "See you again, ma'am."

The woman nodded at him and disappeared inside the gallery door.

"What'd you think was in there, Ezrah? An Uzi — or maybe a bomb?" Becker barked out a short, nasty laugh.

Ezrah felt his face grow hot under the man's gaze. "Just make sure you check that every time she comes in."

"I always do, *sir*," Becker replied.

Ezrah wheeled around, his back and legs feeling stiff and awkward as he walked toward the guard room under Becker's scrutiny. As he entered the room and relaxed slightly, though, he felt a prick of fear. Becker was not lax; he never had been. But now that he had warned him about looking into the case each time, he might just let it go by the next time out of rebellion against "the nigger's" authority. He had warned Becker about looking only because he had been trying to regain his sense of dignity. Giving in to his pride may have been a serious mistake.

At the coffee machine, he plunked in the correct change, and while he was waiting for the paper cup to fill, he frowned again.

It was something his mother had said about the woman. Or, rather, something she hadn't said. She had described her so accurately that he had been able to pick her out from quite a distance away. The way she looked, even the way she walked. And yet, his mother had never said anything about a case, and Becker said she carried it all the time. It wasn't like his mother to leave out something that would have stood out so clearly. She would have remembered that.

He retrieved the cup from the machine and drank the coffee standing up, a frown still on his face.

PART
FIVE

"All it needs is a minor tune-up," Stephanie said. "Pat and I can do that."

Marian stood beside the Volkswagen and watched Stephanie, who seemed to be poking at something in the engine of the little car. Pat Henderson, a small, feisty black woman who had been their friend for the two years since she had moved from Jacksonville to Saint Augustine, plucked at the fan belt.

Standing beside Marian was Liz Culbertson, a plump woman with ash blonde hair, Pat's lover of six months and a longtime friend of Stephanie and Marian's. She shook her head and gave Marian a look that conveyed disbelief at what she was witnessing.

"I assume you're going to need special tools," Marian said.

Stephanie lifted her head from the engine and smiled. "I suppose it would be easier to do with tools."

Marian turned to Liz with an uplifted eyebrow. "What do you think? Maybe a couple of hundred dollars?"

"Sounds about right."

"No, no, not that much," Stephanie protested. "And even if they did cost that much, it would save us a lot more in the long run, because we can use them over and over."

"They can use them over and over," Marian repeated to Liz, "and it'll save us a lot more."

Liz grinned at Marian's tone. "I'm sure it will."

Pat harrumphed and clapped her hand on Stephanie's shoulder. "Don't pay any attention to them. They don't understand cars." She pushed her thumb against the fan belt. "Did you get that manual?"

"We don't understand cars," Marian said dryly. "I assume that means they do."

Liz tried to stifle a laugh by keeping her mouth closed.

"The manual's on the front seat," Stephanie said.

"Well, I can definitely tell that our assistance is not needed," Marian said. She put her arm around Liz's waist and walked her toward the porch. "I'm glad the hospital's only a few blocks away," she said more loudly, this time over her shoulder. "I can walk if I have to."

Liz guffawed, and Stephanie and Pat looked up for a moment.

Liz sat down on the steps and picked up her glass of iced tea. "Do you believe this?" She tilted the rim of her glass toward Stephanie and Pat and shook her head.

Marian shrugged. "I'm going to ignore it." She took a sip of tea. "Does Pat have any talent at all along these lines?"

"Are you kidding? She tried changing the oil in our car one time, and when she was screwing the oil filter back on, she turned it the wrong way and ended up stripping the threads on the thing that the filter screws on to."

"Wonderful. The extent of Stephanie's knowledge of cars is how to turn one on and where to put the gas." Marian furrowed her brow in seeming concentration. "No, come to think of it, I believe I saw her put a quart of oil in one time."

"So why is she doing this now?"

"God knows," Marian sighed. "I think it has something to do with the fact that she feels frustrated about not being able to do anything about the baby except wait. The other day, I found a library book in the stuff piled on the coffee table. It was about building baby furniture. I asked her about it, and she said she wanted to make something for him, but then everything looked so complicated that she figured she couldn't do it. I think the car thing is just something to keep herself busy."

Liz lifted one eyebrow. "Maybe it's some sort of butch thing."

Marian started to laugh, but she had been trying to swallow a mouthful of tea, and she ended up spraying part of it onto the bushes beside the porch. Stephanie looked toward them with her own uplifted eyebrow, and Marian laughed harder.

"No," Liz said in mock seriousness, "I'm telling you, I think it's a distinct possibility." She jabbed Marian's jeans-clad knee with an index finger. "You know, in the old days, butches had construction jobs, trucking jobs—I mean if it's true that there's a grain of truth even in stereotypes, then the term 'diesel dyke' may have some validity." She pointed her glass toward Stephanie and Pat. "Stephanie's a psychic, Pat's a nurse. Those are not exactly the butchiest jobs in the world, you know. Maybe they feel they have to assert their innate butchiness from time to time."

Marian was still grinning. "You know, of course, that as feminists, we're not supposed to give any credence to role-playing any more."

"Who said anything about playing? I think you ought to be dead serious about it."

Marian laughed so loudly at this that Stephanie looked up with a questioning half-smile. "Are you laughing at us?" she called.

Liz waved her hand at Stephanie. "Go back to your work, you butches. We want that car fixed. We femmes are gonna sit here and relax. Pay no attention to us. We don't understand cars."

Grinning, Stephanie turned back to the manual and looked at the page Pat was showing her.

Liz swirled the rapidly melting ice in her tea. "Is she going to do this for the next five months?"

Marian closed her eyes and groaned. "Dear God, I hope not."

"Well, at least we can hope," Liz said. "So, on to you. How have you been feeling lately?"

"Fine. The usual complaints, of course. I had morning sickness early on, my ankles swell, and I seem to have less patience than usual. I dropped a clay flower pot the other day and started crying. The damned thing couldn't have been worth more than a quarter. I think I got it at a yard sale. When I'm not crying, I'm being a bitch. I don't know how Stephanie puts up with me."

Liz chuckled. "You're entitled. Your hormones are weirding out."

"Mmm." Marian was silent for a moment. "You know, I've heard that a couple of our sisters have said some rather hard things about my keeping this child. They seem offended that I'd even consider it."

"I heard something like that the other day."

"Yeah?"

Liz took another sip of tea. "Yeah."

"So give. What's the latest gossip?"

"Well, I believe I heard that one or two people have said that you're assisting the enemy by keeping a child that was conceived during a rape."

"You're kidding."

"Nope."

Marian took a deep breath and released it. "You know, the funny thing is, I almost understand where they're coming from." She stabbed a finger on the step for emphasis. "I am not, however, going to allow my anger at a rapist to stop Stephanie and me from having a child." She glanced at Liz. "Could I tell you something?"

"I hope you know you don't have to explain anything to *me*."

Marian gave Liz a half-smile. "Maybe that's why I want to." She looked away, her voice soft, hesitant. "A long time

·136·

ago, one night just after Stef and I had made love, I was overwhelmed by this—yearning to have her child. At that moment, it didn't matter that it was physically impossible. It didn't matter that the feeling might be seen by some as politically incorrect, that it might be seen as a yearning for a heterosexual role—that what I really wanted was a man. Nothing mattered except that—in the deepest part of my being—I wanted to have Stephanie's child." She took a deep breath, released it, and looked at Liz again. "You sure it's okay to talk about this?"

"It's very okay," Liz said quietly.

Marian glanced toward Stephanie. "It made no sense, Liz, it just was. The anger at the injustice—the feeling of loss was incredible. I cried my heart out that night. Stephanie held me and cried with me. I don't think I had ever loved her any more than right then." Marian felt Liz's comforting hand on her back, and she cleared her throat.

"Anyway, after that, we talked about having a child. How it would be our child." She paused. "We've wanted that for a long time now. It just never seemed to be the right time. I guess maybe it never is. Then, after I was raped, when I found out I was pregnant—" She shook her head. "I could have had an abortion, Liz. I thought about that, of course. But where would that have left us? Back at square one, basically. We could adopt a child—maybe, and that's a big maybe—or we could have gone the route of artificial insemination. But it seemed ludicrous to do either of those things. After all, I found out I was pregnant when I was already a month and a half along. To have an abortion and then start all over seemed stupid. And, after all, the kid I'm going to have in five months or so isn't the person who raped me."

Liz set the glass on the step and was quiet for a moment. "His father did, though, and he was more than just a little psychotic. It's funny. The prevalent idea used to be that it was all in the genes. Then the humanistic approach came along—environment was everything. Now we seem to have come full circle. Genes are becoming popular again."

"I think the idea that it's a combination is probably more likely. Say Talbot had an unnatural aggressiveness—a tendency to violence that erupted into a psychosis because of his background. Maybe—"

"Do you know a lot about his background?"

"A fair amount. Dempsey—the sheriff in Johnson—knew Talbot all his life, and he filled us in. Basically, Talbot's mother ran away when he was a small child because she couldn't take the abuse from his father. She didn't take the boy with her because she believed her husband would find her and kill her. He convinced the boy that it was her fault and then spent the rest of his life poisoning the kid's mind with how all women deserved to be abused."

"And the innate aggressiveness—the genes part?"

Marian smiled. "I suspect every military general or high-powered business executive or even politician has had what could be called an unusual level of aggressiveness."

"I suspect that's true," Liz said. She picked up the glass again and leaned back against the step. "Well, even if you were the kind of person to worry about what others think, I wouldn't spend a lot of time agonizing over the opinions of a couple of our so-called sisters who may or may not be living in the real world. You have a lot of friends who are very happy for both of you."

"Thanks," Marian said quietly. She patted Liz's knee. "I know that's true, but sometimes it helps to hear it."

The telephone rang, and Marian got up to answer it, but before she went into the house, she turned to Liz. "By the way, it feels good to have a friend I could tell that to."

Liz gave Marian a gentle smile. "It feels good to have a friend who trusts me that much."

A few minutes later, Marian appeared on the porch again and motioned to Stephanie, then she went back to the telephone.

"What is it?" Stephanie appeared in the doorway, wiping her hands on a grimy towel.

Marian covered the receiver with her hand. "It's Helen. She's almost hysterical. She found a gun in Woody's car yesterday. While you talk to her, I'll pack our things."

"Our things?"

Marian handed her the receiver. "You think you're going without me, butch?"

Stephanie grinned and leaned over to give Marian a quick kiss. "Then go pack," she whispered. "When I get off the phone, I'll tell Pat and Liz."

FRIDAY
3
NOVEMBER
1989

From the northwest of Atlanta, from the Tennessee border, Interstate 75 makes its way into the city and then exits into the rest of Georgia for its shoot down the west coast of Florida. From the northeast, from South Carolina, Interstate 85 winds into the city and leaves to be on its way to Montgomery, Alabama. In the middle of Atlanta, the two join for a stretch in what Atlantans call the Downtown Connector. Interstate 20 cuts east-west across the center.

Few stretches of road in the South have been so maligned for the past twenty years as the Connector, and it's one reason why visitors are apt to say about the Empire City of the South, "Atlanta will be a wonderful city when they finish it." Traffic moves faster than it should, as a rule, except during the so-called rush hour, which usually lasts for a minimum of three hours in the morning and evening on weekdays. During rush hour, traffic crawls through the heart of the city, with a great deal of sweating, swearing, and exhaust fumes.

It was at five-thirty, during the middle of just such a rush hour, that Stephanie, Marian, and Helen found themselves in bumper-to-bumper, fifteen-mile-an-hour traffic on the Connector.

"I keep getting something about gold. I don't know what." Stephanie put the car into neutral and kept her foot on the brake. Traffic was getting into what more than one radio announcer was fond of calling "stop-and-slow."

"Gold?" Helen frowned. She sat in the back seat, her hands twisted together in her lap, wondering what was going on. They had been driving through the downtown streets and had been on and off the interstates for two hours now. Once in a while, Stephanie would pull the car onto a side street and sit for a few minutes, her eyes closed, not saying anything. Then, her eyes would open, and she would say to Marian, "Nothing." Once, near the apartment where Woody had lived previously, Stephanie had turned around with a frown on her face and asked if Helen knew the neighborhood. When Helen told Stephanie where Woody had lived, Stephanie had nodded and said, almost as if she had been talking to herself, "Good. At least that means I'm picking her up." Whatever that had meant, Helen thought.

"And old men."

Helen started at Stephanie's voice. No one had said anything for several minutes.

"I know it sounds strange," Stephanie said, "but that's what I keep seeing. Gold and old men." She looked at Marian and shrugged.

A few minutes later, they crawled around a curve and crept under I-20. As they exited the overpass, Stephanie had her head turned to the right and was talking to Marian. Between the edge of the overpass, as she left it, and the beginning of a building that followed closely upon it, a sudden flash of gold filled her vision. She swiveled toward it, her heart lurching in her chest. The right tires went off the road, and she jerked the steering wheel back. The driver in the car behind her blew his horn. Marian bumped against the window and stared at her.

"Sorry," Stephanie said. "Are you okay?" She saw Marian nod, and she turned to Helen, who was righting herself in the backseat. "You?" As she saw Helen nod as well, she breathed a sigh of relief.

Finding that she was just several yards from the next exit, she left the interstate traffic and braked to a stop as soon as she could find a driveway. The concrete, windowless building that housed the Georgia State Archives sat to her right. Almost directly straight ahead, gold glinted in the sunlight.

"My God," she breathed, "that's it." She turned to Marian. "That's the Capitol, right?"

"That's the Capitol," Marian responded. "What do you mean, 'That's it'?"

Stephanie looked back at Helen. "Can you see it from your apartment—through that casement window?"

Helen hesitated for a moment and then nodded.

Stephanie stared at the Capitol. "I can't believe this. Every time we come into Atlanta, we pass it. I guess I just got so used to seeing it that I didn't see it any more."

She put the car in gear again and threaded her way through the maze of streets surrounding the imposing structure until she ended up on Trinity Avenue. Pulling into an empty parking space in the left-hand curb lane of the one-way street, her gaze was drawn to the small park at her left.

"What do you think Woody's going to do?" Helen's voice was husky.

Stephanie frowned and avoided looking at her. "I'm not sure yet. I think she's still in the planning stage. I don't think even she knows for sure when she's going to do it."

"What are you going to do when you find out?"

Marian turned in the front seat. "Helen," she said gently, "you must realize that when we know something definite, we're going to have to contact the authorities."

Helen stiffened. "What do you mean, 'contact the authorities'?"

Marian glanced at Stephanie and then turned again to Helen. "Helen, we keep trying to tell you. Woody is planning something very dangerous. She bought a gun. You can't expect us not to try to stop her."

"Woody's a good person," Helen said. "I thought you were going to try to help her."

"Nobody can help her, Helen, unless she allows it."

Tears pooled in Helen's eyes. "She won't." She turned toward the window, and her voice was barely audible. "I lost Katie. Now I'm going to lose Woody, too." No one said anything, and after a minute, she took a deep breath and squared her shoulders. Her voice was stronger when she looked at Marian again. "I guess I'm feeling sorry for myself."

Marian gave her a small smile. "You've got a right to feel that way. It's a hard thing that we're asking you to do."

Helen frowned. "What you're asking me to do?" She shook her head. "You don't understand. I've told you. I have no intention of doing what you want if that means committing Woody to a state mental institution."

"A state institution is not necessarily what has to be done. Atlanta has a lot of community mental-health centers that can help her," Marian said.

Helen laughed shortly. "Oh, no. No. I had a roommate once who decided to go bananas, and her therapist told me to take her to the community mental-health center. She didn't get better after a few weeks, and even though she signed herself in, the center had the right after that period to transfer her to the Georgia Mental Health Institute." She shook her head more vigorously. "I saw her in there. I will not see Woody in there. I can't." She paused for a moment, and when she spoke again, her tone of voice conveyed the message that the subject was closed. "Besides that," she said softly, "Woody would never make it that far. She would kill herself first."

Marian sighed and looked at Stephanie with a question in her eyes.

Stephanie ran her fingers through her hair and turned to stare out the window at the Capitol once more.

The Three Sisters Restaurant on Matanzas Boulevard was as busy at one-thirty in the afternoon as it had been at noon, when Marian and Stephanie had driven by the first time and decided to do a few errands and return. The hum of diners, silverware, and sounds from the kitchen, as well as the aroma of freshly prepared seafood, filled the large, rustic-looking dining room.

Stifling a yawn with the back of her hand, Stephanie shook out her napkin and put it in her lap. She looked at her plate of seafood. "I don't know if I can keep my head up long enough to eat."

Marian glanced at her watch. "Maybe we should suggest they start taking reservations. I expect this during the tourist season, but not at this time of the year."

Stephanie picked up her fork and speared a shrimp. "Did you have something planned for this afternoon?"

"I had thought I might get some writing done while I'm on my leave of absence. It seemed like a good time to do it, but I'm not getting anything done." She saw Stephanie's look. "And don't tell me I don't have to go traipsing around the country with you. That's not the issue."

"Mmm."

Marian glanced at her and picked up a slice of lemon. "That's a really profound comment, dear." She squeezed the lemon into a glass of sweetened iced tea, and it slipped from her fingers and plopped onto the red-and-white checkered table-cloth. "Damn," she muttered softly.

Stephanie looked up with the beginning of a smile. "What's wrong?"

Marian picked up the lemon and threw it into the tea. Her voice held a stronger note of irritation. "Why does something have to be wrong?"

"No reason. You just seem to be a bit on edge."

Marian gazed at her for a moment, then the corner of her mouth twitched as she tried to stifle a laugh. "A bit on edge? How about a bitch on wheels?" The laugh won. She reached across the table and put her hand on Stephanie's. "Sorry. I've been a crab all day, and I know you're tired, too, sweetheart." She smiled. "And I guess my hormones are 'weirding out' again, as Liz puts it."

Stephanie chuckled. "I suppose."

They ate in silence for a few minutes before Stephanie spoke again.

"You know, this is beginning to seem like a Three Stooges movie."

"What is?"

"The way we keep going to Atlanta and coming home, and then going back to Atlanta and coming home. Racing around without accomplishing anything."

"That's true." Marian lifted a hot, lightly browned hush puppy and crunched into it. After a moment, she said, "By the way, what did you see at the Capitol?"

Stephanie sighed. "The same thing as in the nightmares, really. Besides that, there's just the feeling of a lot of fear with a lot of power behind it."

"Whose?"

Stephanie glanced up. "Whose?"

Marian nodded, her mouth full. "Mmm. Whose fear?" The words were muffled.

"I don't know. It's strange. I hadn't really thought about it." Stephanie sat stock-still for a moment, a frown playing across her face. Her eyes seemed to be staring in space. Then she blinked and gazed at Marian.

"Someone sitting on a platform, behind a podium of some kind." She paused. "The person the gun is aimed at—but not the one who's in the most danger."

Marian lifted her eyebrows. "That's interesting."

"Really." Stephanie was still frowning.

"Look," Marian said softly, "don't you think it's time to tell someone about this? The police, for instance?"

"Tell them what?" The frown was gone, and Stephanie had started on the stuffed crab.

"Déjà vu," Marian muttered. "We seem to have only one conversation." She picked up her fork, fiddled with it for a second, and then tapped it on the table, looking at Stephanie intently. "You've got to tell someone what you saw. If you're still thinking nobody would listen, you're forgetting that there are a lot of influential people who would believe you."

"She hasn't done anything. Not yet. And before you say we ought to talk to Woody herself, if we told her that we know what she's planning, she'd just put it on hold. She's put it on hold for a long time now. She'd just wait longer. I've got a feeling that now that she's decided what to do, she can probably wait a very long time. She's setting up everything in her head now—getting it all worked out." She shook her head slightly. "If we scare her off, it'll give her even more time to set it up so that it works the way she wants it to. It's still going to be a while before it happens. If we let her do it in the time frame she wants to, I think we've got a chance to stop her. If we interfere now and she puts it off, we won't be in a position to stop her."

Marian sighed. "Okay. Whatever you say, sweetheart. I guess it's just hard to wait for whatever's going to happen."

She hesitated. "And I'm worried about the baby."

Stephanie patted her hand. "Don't. I told you, everything's going to be all right." She smiled. "Believe me."

Marian nodded, then she looked at Stephanie and smiled. "Actually, I'm probably just trying to get some attention by appealing to your sympathy. The truth is that I'm as healthy as a horse, and you know it. A hundred years ago, I'd drop the kid in the field and finish picking the row afterwards."

Stephanie laughed out loud. "Well, I know you're taking care of yourself, but I think that might be a bit overstated."

"I suppose," Marian grinned. But after a moment, she sobered. "You know, there *is* something I'd like to know, though."

"And what might that be?"

"Are you keeping something from me?"

"Why would you think that?" Marian continued to look at Stephanie, who was staring intently at her plate, fork in hand, suddenly absorbed in her shrimp. "I just wonder if you know more than what you're telling me. It wouldn't be the first time you tried to protect me."

She watched Stephanie carefully, and when she got no response, she sighed and turned back to her plate. They ate in silence for several minutes again before Stephanie pushed her plate to one side and leaned back in her chair.

"Marian—" Stephanie picked up her cigarettes, shook one out, and lit it before she continued. "I really didn't want to worry you."

Marian rolled her eyes upward. "When are you going to learn that I get a lot more worried when I know something's going on and you don't tell me what it is?"

Stephanie sighed. "When I told you about the boy being with this man—" She stopped.

"Give. It's worse than what you've said."

Stephanie shook her head. "I don't know. I wonder whether I'm involved in this because of the child, or if I'm *supposed* to be involved in this thing, so I'm being shown that the child will be affected by the outcome of it so I'll involve myself."

Marian lifted her eyebrows. "Well, that does seem rather convoluted. Do you mean that you think somebody up there—" she pointed her finger toward the ceiling, "or wherever—is orchestrating this whole thing and giving you a reason to get involved by showing you something that might not be real?"

Stephanie gave her a small smile. "You know, sometimes when you say out loud something that I've been thinking, it sounds different."

Marian rolled her eyes again. "I'll bet." She frowned. "Well, have you ever had that experience before?"

Stephanie shook her head.

"Then I think we'd have to assume that it's not happening this time. I think we have to assume that if it's something you're seeing quite clearly, then it's real. Or it will be."

Stephanie sighed. "I suppose."

"That's not all of it. Like I said—give."

Stephanie brushed her hand through her hair and stared out the window at the traffic going down Matanzas Boulevard. "You were there, too."

"I was where, too?"

"When I saw the three-year-old boy with the man kneeling beside him—that first time. You were there with them."

Marian had started to lift the glass of iced tea, but when it was halfway to her mouth, she set it down. "I don't understand what that means."

Stephanie tapped ashes off the cigarette and then looked up. "I think something's going to happen to you and the boy. At some time in the future. I don't know what. But I think the man I keep seeing is going to be instrumental in saving your life some day." She held Marian's eyes. "If he dies — if Woody kills him—" She stopped and looked away for a moment. "I don't know when. I don't know how. But I do believe it will happen." Without warning, tears began pooling in Stephanie's eyes, and she wiped them away with the back of her hand.

"Jesus," Marian breathed, "you've been holding all this inside of you?"

Stephanie continued as if Marian had not spoken, as if the words had piled up and had to come out all at once. "When we were at the Capitol, all of a sudden, I found myself in a hospital room with this man. His head was bandaged, and there was an IV hanging beside the bed. While I was standing there, the monitor that shows the heartbeat went flat."

Marian's voice was shaky. "Do you think he's going to die?"

Stephanie shook her head and looked toward the street again. "I don't know," she said quietly. "I really don't know."

Marian propped her elbow on the table and looked down at the table. Her voice was soft, but the shakiness was gone. "Damn," she said. A moment later, she reached up and brushed away tears from her own cheeks. "I guess I've been avoiding thinking about what might happen three or four years from now. I assumed we could cross that bridge when we came to it. All of a sudden, it seems very close."

Stephanie reached across the table, took Marian's hand, and squeezed it gently. "It doesn't necessarily mean that he's going to die, remember."

Marian nodded her head. "I know, sweetheart," she whispered. "I know."

The rest of their meal, what they ate of it, was eaten in silence.

Charles Becker saw the woman with the trombone case coming down the hall and smiled to himself. She was another chance to get a little more even with the nigger they had promoted over him last year.

It should have been his job. He had been here longer. A lot longer. And he'd had real training for the job—military training. Hell, he thought sometimes when he saw Palmer bossing the other guards around, the nigger had only gone to a namby-pamby security-guard school.

So he took every chance that was presented to him to undermine Palmer's authority. It was the only way he had to get back at him—at all of them who had told him Palmer was the "best man for the job" when they passed him over for the promotion. Even if it was just getting back a little bit.

He caught himself grinding his teeth and tried to relax. Just thinking about the whole thing pissed him off all over again. But he was going to get back at them just that little bit whenever he could. He smiled. With this girl and her trombone, it would never matter.

She approached him, gave him that funny smile she always did, and put the case down on the floor. He watched her, and when she started to pop open the latches, he touched her shoulder.

"Hey," he said softly, "there ain't no need to do that, now is there?"

She looked up at him. "You don't want me to open it?"

"Naw," Becker drawled, flashing his teeth. "Tell you the truth, I get kind of tired of looking at the same thing all the time, you know?" He chuckled and then winked at her. "I mean, you don't have a bomb in there, do you?"

Woody looked down at the case, back up at the guard, and smiled. "No, I don't guess so."

"Well, that's what I thought." Becker grinned at her.

Woody bent to secure the latches and, knowing the guard couldn't see her face, smiled triumphantly. She picked up the case, gave him a polite smile and a nod of thanks, and walked past him into the gallery.

PART
SIX

1

Woody shivered and reached to turn the heat up in the car. With the warmth, though, came drowsiness, and after just a few minutes, she turned the heat down again.

She could deal with the discomfort, she thought. In a matter of hours, she would have Katie back home. She smiled as she thought of how Helen's face would look when she first saw Katie. Lit up, happy, the way it used to look before the cancer had started eating into their lives.

She looked down at the speedometer and pushed the car up to seventy. Night closed in as the sign for State Highway 24 appeared ahead.

2

Awaking cold, Marian found that the sheet and both blankets had been pulled off. Next to her, wrapped in the sheet and blankets, mummy style, Stephanie was moaning softly in her sleep.

Marian sighed and began disengaging the covers carefully, trying not to wake her lover. That accomplished, she snuggled next to Stephanie and stroked her back. After a few minutes, Stephanie quieted, and Marian put her arm around her waist to hold her close.

3

Half a block from where she thought the house was, Woody cut the lights and engine of the Toyota and coasted down the gentle slope of the street until she found a mailbox with the address on it. Braking to a stop, she waited a moment, listening and watching. There were a lot of streetlights in the Chicago suburb, but large oak trees and thickly planted, tall bushes screening immaculately manicured lawns from their neighbors meant little light except in the street itself.

Getting out of the car, she quickly trotted up the driveway, where a late-model Honda sat, and found cover behind the shrubbery next to the house. She crept noiselessly along the side of the house and, reaching a window, tried to push it open and had no luck. She made her way around the back and to the other side of the house. Finding no entrance and deciding that the front windows were too dangerous, she circled back to the patio in the rear.

French doors led off the flagstone pavement. As she turned to make sure no one could see her from the back of the property, she bumped into a lawn chair. The metal grated across the stones, and she stood still, her breath white in the crisp air. She listened for long minutes, but when she heard nothing, she made her way more carefully to the doors.

She shoved her hands into her pockets and found the glass cutter and masking tape. Moving as quickly as possible, she made a heavy, four-inch vertical score in the panel next to the door handle and put two pieces of tape across it. Making three more scores to complete a square, she taped each side in turn, then rapped the square sharply. It popped loose and was held lightly by the tape. It took only a moment to lift out the square of glass and reach in to open the door. By the time she was finished, her fingers were numb with cold.

A few minutes later, she had found Katie's room, where the illumination from a nightlight spilled into the hallway. As she stood in the hall, looking in, she smiled. The teddy bear she and Helen had sent Katie for Christmas was tucked under her arm, and her mouth was open slightly in heavy sleep. She went and sat on the edge of the bed and touched Katie's cheek. As the little girl came awake, her eyes widened when she saw Woody. She opened her mouth to speak, and Woody placed an index finger across her lips.

"Shh. We must be very quiet."

"Woody," Katie exclaimed in a whisper. She threw her arms around Woody's neck and hugged her tightly. Then she looked around. "Is Mommy here?"

"I'm going to take you to her. But you must be very quiet, okay?"

"Is Daddy going, too?"

Woody's eyes narrowed, and then she shook her head. "No. He needs to sleep. But he knows where you're going."

She stood up and looked around in the dim light. Spotting a dresser across the room, she went to it and found Katie's clothes. "Do you have a suitcase in here, Katie?"

Katie nodded her head vigorously and pointed toward the closet.

It took only a short time to get Katie bundled into warm clothes and pack a few things into the suitcase, then Woody picked her up in one arm and picked up the suitcase with the other.

Halfway down the hall, Katie whispered, "Wait, Woody. I forgot Teddy."

"Okay," Woody whispered in return. "Just be quiet, okay?"

Katie nodded her head, and Woody put her down and watched as she ran on her tiptoes back up the hall.

As she waited, Woody noticed that she was standing near another open door. She looked in and saw Douglas Corwin lying sprawled in the middle of a king-size bed, asleep. She frowned, put the suitcase down in the hallway, and moved to stand in the doorway.

Reaching down next to her leg, she picked up the rifle, brought it to her shoulder, and once again felt the cool stock against her cheek. In the beginning, it was a frightening sensation to have that much power next to her skin. Now, it was a comforting feeling.

Light filtered into the room from the window across the room, and she could see his head clearly in the cross hairs. Small, blond hairs stuck out from behind his ear. The back of his neck was broad. In her mind's eye, she saw the triumphant smile he had shot her across the courtroom that terrible day when he and the others had taken Katie away.

She began to squeeze the trigger very, very slowly.

4

Half asleep, Marian rolled over toward the middle of the bed and reached out her hand. When it encountered nothing beside her, she opened her eyes sleepily. She sighed and ran her hands through her hair and, after a minute, swung her legs over the side of the bed and sat up. Finding her nightgown under the covers, she pulled it over her head and made her way to the kitchen.

Stephanie was sitting at the table, a cigarette in her hand. The tip glowed in the darkness among the shadows created by the faint moonlight that filtered through the curtains and fell across the kitchen table.

"Any particular reason you're sitting in the dark?"

"I didn't want to wake you." Stephanie stubbed out the cigarette.

Marian walked up behind her and put her arms around Stephanie's chest and laid her head on the top of Stephanie's. "You could have just closed the door."

"I guess I don't need much light for thinking."

"Thinking — or worrying?"

Stephanie chuckled. "I keep asking if you're sure I'm the psychic. Sometimes I don't think I can keep anything from you."

"Would you like to keep more from me?"

Stephanie shook her head slightly and put her hand on Marian's arm. "No," she said softly. "I find it a great comfort that you can know me so well and still love me."

"The more I know about you, the more I love you."

"I wouldn't think there would be anything more to know after all these years."

Marian smiled in the darkness and buried her face in Stephanie's hair. Stephanie's fragrance and warmth engulfed her. "Oh, I learn something new about you every once in a while, my friend. Something new and wonderful."

Stephanie laughed softly. "New and wonderful?"

"Mmm."

"Like what?"

"Like how you always put on your left sock and then your left shoe and then your right sock and then your right shoe."

Stephanie laughed loudly, pushed her chair back, and pulled Marian down onto her lap.

Marian leaned back slightly, still smiling, and pushed Stephanie's hair back from her forehead. "I'm almost five and a half months pregnant. I'm too heavy for you now."

"Never."

Marian took Stephanie's face in her hands and kissed her warmly. "I'm going to turn the light on and make us some tea."

"That sounds good."

As Marian put the tea kettle on to boil and turned back toward Stephanie, she frowned. Stephanie's face was haggard and drawn from lack of sleep. Dark circles lay under her eyes. She looked as if she were losing weight.

"You need to eat more, dear. You're looking thin."

Stephanie lit another cigarette. "I know. I'll try." There was a long pause. "You know what I keep wondering?"

"What?"

"Why does the subconscious mind — the right brain — always talk to me in symbols?"

"Obviously, dear, because that's its language."

Stephanie harrumphed and tapped an ash off the cigarette. "But that's my whole problem. It always talks in symbols." She sighed. "All these symbols. These goddamned symbols. Why can't the right brain—" she slapped her hand down on the table, "be like the left brain?"

Marian cocked an eyebrow in Stephanie's direction. It always surprised her when Stephanie swore. It was an indication that her frustration level was reaching a peak.

Stephanie sighed again. "When I was a lot younger—"

"From the sound of it, that was about a thousand years ago."

Stephanie smiled. "At least. Anyway, since I've never been able to zero in on myself, I decided once — about fifteen years ago, I guess — to have another psychic do a reading for *me*. I was trying to decide whether to get a real job or do this stuff for the rest of my life. Well, the psychic asked me if I were a swimming coach."

Marian guffawed and put the back of her hand to her mouth. "Sorry," she said, but a smile remained.

Stephanie grinned. "Nothing to be sorry about. I laughed when he said it, too. So, I said, 'No, I love to swim, but I've never thought about being a swimming coach.' So he went through a whole list of aquatic jobs, and then when that produced nothing, he started in on other sports. Finally, I asked him to just tell me what it was he saw. As it turned out, he was seeing a cut-away picture of a swimming pool. He saw me on one side of the pool, looking at him, and then I dove in, swam underwater all the way across the pool, surfaced, and then stood and looked at him, smiling." She cocked her head at Marian. "You probably know more than he did what it meant."

Marian shrugged. "Well, it was obviously too literal an interpretation, since that's what we're talking about, so I would assume the water was a symbol for your emotional nature.

Maybe you were going to go through an emotional experience, submerge yourself in it perhaps — and then come out on the other side okay."

"Exactly," Stephanie said. "He was letting the vision through, but he was having a hard time interpreting it because he was being too literal." She frowned. "Maybe I'm being too literal in this case."

"But there's really no way to know, is there?"

"I suppose not. But I really don't see any symbols like the water in this nightmare."

The tea kettle started to whistle, but Marian made no move toward it for a long moment while she held Stephanie's eyes. Finally, she turned and lifted the kettle off the burner. "You know," she said, "there was someone else killed that day, too, although we tend to forget it."

Stephanie frowned. "Was it a secret service agent? You're right, I don't remember."

"What you're remembering is that there was a report at first that a secret service agent was killed, but it turned out to be false." Marian put the mugs on the table, dangled a tea bag in each, and reached for the kettle. Pouring steaming water over the tea bags, she said, "The one killed was a Dallas police officer. Apparently he met up with Oswald after Oswald left the book depository, and he stopped him because he fit the description of the man they were looking for."

"And he was killed. I remember that now."

"Mmm."

Stephanie frowned again. "I wonder what his name was."

Marian shrugged. "No idea. Think it might be important?"

"I doubt it. It's probably just one more thing that confuses the issue."

"Sorry."

Marian watched as Stephanie put out her cigarette, and then she frowned. Stephanie was grabbing her head, rocking back and forth, as if she were in agony. Marian rushed to her.

"Stef, what is it?"

"I don't know," she gasped. "I feel like my head is going to explode."

"Do you see anything?"

"I — I just see a lot of lights. Like an explosion."

Marian put her arms around Stephanie and held her tightly. After a minute, Stephanie was still, and Marian saw her eyes fly open.

"My God," Stephanie whispered. She ran her fingers through her hair. "I was so stuck on the idea that she was waiting for an opportunity to do whatever she wanted to do at the Capitol, I never even thought about Helen's little girl."

Marian took a deep breath and released it. "You mean Woody's going after Katie?"

"I think she already has her." Stephanie got up and headed for the telephone on the wall beside the back door.

"Who are you calling?"

"Helen." Stephanie leafed through several small pieces of paper that were lying on the countertop below the telephone and apparently found the one she wanted. She dialed a number, her hand shaking slightly.

"Answer, damn it," Stephanie whispered through clenched teeth. After what seemed like minutes, she turned and hung up the receiver. "There's no answer."

"What now?"

"The only thing we can do is wait."

For the next few minutes, Stephanie paced and smoked, while Marian sat quietly at the table, saying little.

5

Helen awoke with the ringing of the telephone, but it seemed to take a great deal of effort and time to turn over in bed to face the nightstand on which the telephone sat. Her limbs felt as heavy as stones, and lifting a hand toward the receiver presented an impossible task.

It continued to ring. With almost willpower alone, she inched her hand toward the ringing and only succeeded in knocking over the bottle of sleeping pills she had left there just as she went to bed.

She had not slept for more than two or three hours a night in the past three days, and she had known that if she were to cope with what was going on in her life, she would have to have sleep. The mild calming of the pills had been enough to put her into a deep sleep early in the evening.

She made another effort to reach the receiver and once again failed.

Can't do it, she thought. Can't do it. She fell back into a deep sleep.

6

"Whatcha doin', Woody?"

Woody turned and saw Katie in the doorway. She was staring at her, the teddy bear in her arms and a puzzled look on her face. Woody put a finger to her lips.

"Nothing," she whispered with a smile.

Putting down the rifle, she picked up the child in one arm and took her into the hallway. Then she retrieved the suitcase with her free hand and started back down the hall.

7

Noticing that Stephanie had stopped pacing, Marian looked up. Stephanie was staring into space.

"Stef?"

Stephanie relaxed visibly. "It's over for now," she said quietly.

"Am I going to stay with you and Mommy forever now, Woody?"

Woody grinned at Katie, who was bundled up in a blanket beside her. She put an arm around her and held her close.

"Forever," Woody said. She turned back to look down the long, dark road in front of them. "Forever," she repeated softly.

"Good," Katie mumbled sleepily.

"Yep, that is good. Now you go to sleep for a while, okay? We've got quite a ways to go. We're going to stay at a motel tomorrow night, and then you'll be home with Mommy the next night. Won't that be nice?"

Katie nodded and moved away from Woody only a bit to snuggle down in the blanket again. In just seconds, she was deeply asleep, the teddy bear held fast in her arms.

1

"How'd you like to go to a movie tonight?"

"Mmm," Stephanie murmured. She turned another page of the national-news section, folded it back, and laid it beside her plate.

Marian took a bite of buttered toast and then lowered the newspaper she was holding in front of her and looked at the toast. "You know, this stuff isn't too bad, but I don't care what they call it, I can tell very easily that it's not butter."

"Mmm."

Marian folded the entertainment section and dropped it on the floor beside the kitchen table. "You have the state news?"

"Mmm." Stephanie lifted the section she was looking at and handed another section across the table.

Marian took the last piece of her bacon and folded it into the other piece of whole-wheat toast on her plate. While she was eating it, she spotted a small news article at the bottom of the front page. "You know," she said, "it's time for us to get another déjà vu speech from the governor this week."

"Hmm?"

"He's giving the State of the State address again. The damned thing is always the same every time."

"Mmm."

"I guess we'll get to hear once more about how the lottery is making our schools so much better. It says here that—"

"What?"

"I said, I'm sure he'll talk about the lottery and how much it's helped—"

"No."

Marian looked up and raised an eyebrow. "No what?"

"They do it all about the same time, don't they?"

"Sorry, pal, I'm not tracking you."

"The governors of all the states. Right around the time the president delivers the State of the Union address. It's always on television."

"I believe so. Why?"

Stephanie pushed her chair back and headed for the telephone. "Because that's when she'll do it."

Marian frowned. "Dear, I don't have any idea of what you're talking about."

"Woody." Stephanie picked up the receiver and began dialing.

"You don't mean tomorrow, for God's sake." She frowned. "Are you talking about the governor of Georgia?"

"Tomorrow, yes. I'm not sure it's the governor, though."

"Christ on a roller coaster," Marian muttered. "Whoever's giving you these damned messages could give you a little more time."

"Don't think that hasn't occurred to me from time to time." She sighed and fidgeted for a moment, and then said abruptly, "Helen? Stephanie Nowland. I tried to call you early this morning, but there was no answer. Do you know where Woody is?"

Stephanie heard the wariness in Helen's voice. "She's visiting her brother Jerry in Dallas. Why?"

"Are you sure she's there? Did you talk to her a short time ago?"

"Yes. As a matter of fact, I did. Why?"

"Because I think Woody's gotten Katie. If she—" There was an abrupt, disbelieving laugh from Helen, and Stephanie closed her eyes and shook her head. "I think you need to call your ex-husband."

"No." Helen's voice was steely now. "I'm not going to do that. She doesn't have Katie. That's ridiculous. And I told you, I won't get Woody into trouble. Particularly over something that's so insane."

"She's going to be in trouble anyway. I'm telling you that she has Katie with her."

"And I'm telling you that she's at her brother's house in Dallas, Texas. She called me last night."

"Did you talk to her brother then?"

"No! But I know that's where she was."

"How do you know she wasn't calling you from somewhere else?"

"I just know. She said that's where she was."

"Helen, Woody is getting worse. She's got her mind set on what she's going to do, and nothing's going to shake it. Not even you — especially if she thinks that what she's doing is in your best interest."

"I'm not going to listen to this any more."

The phone clicked in Stephanie's ear, and she slowly turned and hung up the receiver.

"She hung up on you?"

Stephanie nodded.

"Then don't you think it's about time you called Dempsey?" Marian asked.

"I do," Stephanie replied wearily.

2

"Son of a bitch," Harold Donaldson muttered.

The governor's aide sat looking at the notes he had made on the pad in front of him. Monday mornings always seemed to bring out the wackos, but now he had to deal with some hick-town sheriff who said a psychic in Florida had received a message about the governor being in danger. He sighed, rubbed his eyes, and picked up the phone. The first thing to do was to find out if this sheriff was a flake himself.

A call to the sheriff of Fulton County convinced him that this should be taken seriously. He got up and headed for the governor's office, purpose in his step. But long minutes later, he was still trying to convince Governor Robert Prestwood.

Prestwood leaned back in his chair and swiveled around to face Donaldson. He rubbed the long, aquiline nose that had earned him the title of "Hawk" in his college days.

"Harry, what do you want me to do? Call out the state militia? The friggin' National Guard? For God's sake, man, what's it gonna look like when the press gets there and they ask me, 'Governor Prestwood, how come you have all these cops around here?' So I tell them, and they laugh me out of the state."

Donaldson shook his head. "I think this is serious, Governor. Sheriff Dempsey tells me that this psychic was the one who came up with the killer in a murder case in his county, and she also found the maniac who murdered all those old women in Jacksonville a few years ago. She's—"

Prestwood frowned. "Jacksonville? Are we talking Georgia or—"

"Florida. She's apparently right on the money at least most of—"

"And the person who told you that this sheriff in Johnson County is a stand-up guy was Sheriff Peterson of Fulton County, right?"

"Right. And—"

"Sheriff John Peterson, who has hated my guts for the past twenty years. This is the man you're referring to, right?"

"Yes." Donaldson began to feel weary. It was obvious where the conversation was heading.

"Sheriff John Peterson, who'd like nothing more than to see me look like a jackass in front of the entire state." Prestwood shook his head slowly. "Harry, Harry, Harry. You'll learn one day, boy."

Donaldson left the governor's office and said a few choice words as he sat down at his desk again. He fiddled with the papers in front of him for a while, and then he picked up the telephone. When his call was answered, he lowered his voice.

"Ezrah? Harry Donaldson. Meet me in the lobby of the Trinity-Washington Building, okay? I think you need to know something."

3

"Do you think they'll take care of it?" Marian stood behind Stephanie, who was sitting in a chair at the kitchen table, and massaged her shoulders.

"I assume so. Anyway, there's really nothing much we can do about it now. We just have to trust that they'll handle it all right."

"And what if they don't?" Marian said quietly.

"I don't know," Stephanie responded. She reached up, took Marian's hand, and squeezed it. "I just don't know."

4

That night, Helen sat in the window seat, looking toward the small gold dome of the Georgia State Capitol building in the distance. She had been sitting there for hours, thinking about what she had seen Woody doing at this window, thinking about what Stephanie and Marian had been telling her. The truth, she decided, was that no matter what she believed about Woody, she was going to have to do something when Woody returned. Maybe Woody had money left from the trip to Dallas, and they could go see Katie.

Helen shook her head. Why had Woody even gone there? Especially without saying anything — just leaving in the middle of the night with a note left on the kitchen table. Especially when they didn't even have enough money to pay all the bills this month.

She became aware that tears were wet on her cheeks, and she brushed them away. When Woody got home, they'd talk. But right now, she was tired. So tired.

She looked across the room at the telephone for perhaps the twentieth time in the past couple of hours. Maybe if she called Jerry now, Woody would be there and they could talk. She continued to stare at the telephone, and after a few minutes, she realized why it was taking her so long to make the call.

She was afraid. She was afraid that Stephanie was right — that Woody wasn't there and had never been there.

Sighing heavily, she stood and went to the phone. She heard eight rings before Jerry answered.

"Jerry? This is Helen. Could I speak to Woody, please?"

There was a short silence before the voice on the other end of the line said, "Helen, she's not here. You just missed her again."

Helen hesitated. "Did she ever get there, Jerry?"

There was a longer silence, and then Jerry laughed nervously. "Hey, Helen, she just went out for a while. I think she went over to visit Katherine, that's all. She'll probably be there gabbing for hours."

"Have you got her number?"

"Well, yeah, I got her number, of course, but I think Woody said they were going out to eat or something. I'm sure they won't be there."

Helen felt the tears welling up again. The lies were becoming too obvious for her to dismiss them any longer.

"Look, Jerry," she said quietly, "just ask her to call me when she gets in, okay?"

The relief in his voice was evident. "Yeah — yeah, Helen, I'll do that. Listen, you take care, okay?"

"Sure, Jerry. I will. You, too."

Helen hung up the phone and stood there for long minutes, then she picked up the receiver and dialed the number Marian had given her. Only after trying for what seemed like hours did she give up. She went to bed feeling more alone than she had in her life.

Sometime later, she awoke from a dream that someone was in the apartment. She sat up, her heart pounding. She listened intently but heard nothing. Lying back down, she found herself staring at the ceiling.

Finally, she sighed heavily and swung her legs over the side of the bed and sat up. If she couldn't sleep, she might as well get up and read, she thought. Maybe that would help.

She made her way down the hall without turning on the lights. The streetlights outside the apartment were always enough to enable her to see. But when she got near the end of the hallway, just before Katie's room, she saw a dim light on the floor that was coming from Katie's room. The nightlight had not been on since Katie had been gone, and she was sure she had not turned it on. Her stomach jumped slightly.

Moving silently to the door, she looked in. The faint light shone on Katie's sleeping face. Helen stifled a small cry. Moving closer to the bed, she saw a piece of paper on the floor by the bed and picked it up. She frowned as she read it.

My dear Helen — Katie is where she belongs. With her mother. Now I've got to make things safe for us. Whatever happens, remember I love you. — Woody

"Oh, Woody," Helen breathed. "What have you done?" She put her hands up to her face and stared at Katie. "What have you done?"

5

"What time is it?"

Marian pulled her sleeve back to look at her watch. "Three-thirty." She pushed her sleeve back down and reached in the back seat of the VW for the blanket she had grabbed on their way out the door. "You know, maybe for your birthday, I'll get the heat fixed for you."

"That would be nice." Stephanie took her hand off the wheel and rubbed her eyes. "How much longer, do you think?"

"Well, at the pace you're going, if we don't get stopped for speeding, I'd say about another five hours." She looked at Stephanie carefully. "But I also think it's time to stop and get coffee and walk around for a minute."

"Do we have enough time?"

"There's going to have to be enough time, dear. You're not going to make it otherwise."

A sudden coughing noise from the engine caused Marian to glance at Stephanie. "I wish we could have brought my car."

Stephanie nodded. "I do, too. But it would've been harder to break into Green's Auto Repair than to take mine."

"I suppose," Marian sighed. "Do you think we're going to make it?"

"I think," Stephanie said, "that we're doing all we can." She was silent for a moment. "I just wish I had known a little earlier than this that we might have to stop her ourselves."

"Maybe it was supposed to happen this way," Marian said softly. She turned and stared out the window at the blackness rushing by.

"Maybe," Stephanie responded just as softly.

PART
SEVEN

FRIDAY

12

JANUARY

1990

1

"George! Stand still, for heaven's sake. How can you expect me to tie this thing with you wiggling around like you're six years old?"

"Sorry." George Fowler made an effort to stand still so that Mary could straighten his tie.

She gave the knot a pat. "There." She stood back and looked at him. "You look very nice."

"Thanks." George stuck two fingers down beside his shirt collar and tugged slightly.

"Too tight?"

"No. Not the tie, the collar. I think I'm putting on weight. Not enough exercise."

Mary grinned, put her arms around his waist, and hugged him. "You haven't put on too much weight. I can still get my arms around you."

George chuckled and returned the hug. "You know, I wouldn't be here if it hadn't been for you. I think maybe you should be down on the floor today instead of me. I could watch you from the gallery." He held her at arm's length and looked at her. "How about it?"

Mary laughed. "I'm too blunt. The first time I heard some good ol' boy spouting a racist line, I'd probably get up and punch him in the mouth." She straightened the knot again. "No, you're much more conciliatory than I am. And more realistic. You won't compromise yourself or your ideals, but you'll accept small steps on the way to those ideals. I'd refuse anything but the big prize, and I'd walk away with nothing. You'll end up with the jackpot because you're willing to take the small prizes."

George sighed. "I don't know. I was only here a couple of weeks at the special session, and it looks like there's so much more to do than I thought. Half the time, it seems like nobody's listening, and the rest of the time, it's like they listen and don't care anyway. I was talking to one of 'em about the abortion issue. He had this smug little smirk on his face. He's sure that when it gets brought up in the assembly, all the good ol' boys are gonna see that men get the power back to control their women."

Mary raised her eyebrows. *"Their women?"*

George looked at her. "His words, dear, not mine."

"Thank heavens," Mary said dryly. "I was afraid you were starting to think like they do."

George chuckled. "What? And get my head taken off?"

Mary slapped him on the chest and moved to get her purse on the bed. She picked it up and turned back to him. "And don't you forget it."

"Yes, ma'am," George said, smiling. He went to her and put his arms around her again. "By the way, you're gonna stay with me tonight, aren't you?"

Mary laid her head on his shoulder and nodded her head. "That was nice last night, wasn't it?"

"Mmm."

"I'll stay." She paused. "You know, back in September, I got so lonesome without you. Not just at night, although that was the worst time, but sometimes I'd be working away and, all of a sudden, I'd think of something I wanted to tell you. I even caught myself a time or two getting up to come find you."

George closed his eyes and hugged her tightly. "I know," he whispered. "Me, too. I did the same thing."

Mary smiled. "I know. That's why I got all the phone calls."

"Did you mind?"

"No," Mary said. "It made me know you needed me." She pushed away from him. "Now, Mr. Representative, before I start crying and have to fix my makeup, let's go. I'm looking forward to that fancy omelet you promised me before we have to be at the Capitol."

"Okay. Let me get my briefcase."

"I'll wait for you in the hall."

George nodded and went into the sitting room, where he had set up an office away from the one he had been assigned at the Capitol. As he bent to pick up the briefcase, a bolt of pure agony shot through his head, and he dropped the briefcase. The pain seemed to ricochet back and forth, and he put his hands up to hold his head. A brilliant flash of light accompanied the pain, intensified it. He moaned softly. A moment later, it abated just as suddenly as it had come.

Straightening, he put his hands down, took a deep breath, and composed himself. He heard Mary at the door again, warning him of the time.

He picked up the briefcase, put what he hoped was a smile on his face, and opened the door.

2

Helen opened the door and found Stephanie and Marian standing in the hallway. Her face flooded with relief, and she reached out to touch Marian's arm.

"Thank God you're here. I've been trying to reach you. How did you know?"

Marian stepped through the doorway and started taking off her jacket. "Oh," she said with a small smile, "we have ways of knowing."

A puzzled look appeared on Helen's face, and a look of comprehension followed it. "I suppose I'm pretty dense sometimes, but I've been trying so hard to believe you're wrong." She looked at Stephanie. "I really am sorry."

Stephanie waved her hand. "Don't worry about it."

"No, don't worry about it at all," Marian said. "I don't believe it myself half the time."

Helen gave them a half-smile, but it was fleeting. "I don't know what to do. I've had the phone off the hook all morning except when I was trying to call you, because I'm afraid my ex-husband is going to call, and I don't know what to tell him. I don't want Woody to get into trouble, but I don't know what to do."

"Woody's taking Katie is the least of her troubles now, I'm afraid," Stephanie said quietly. "Look, Helen, we called to get help, but I think there's been a hitch. We're going to have to see if we can stop her ourselves. I'd like you to come with me—"

There was no hesitation in Helen's voice. "Should I get a neighbor to watch Katie?"

Stephanie had been avoiding looking at Marian. "I'd like Marian to stay with her."

"I beg your pardon?" Marian's voice held a tone of slight disbelief.

"Look, I just think it would be better if you stayed here. There's no reason for—"

"Right. If you think, Stephanie Nowland, that you can—"

"Stay here. Please. Do this for me." She took Marian's hands and squeezed them tightly. "Please."

Marian stared at Stephanie for a moment, but she finally sighed in resignation. "Okay. You got it."

A look of relief passed over Stephanie's face. "Thank you."

Marian put her arms around Stephanie and hugged her tightly. "Take care of yourself. I love you."

"I'll be okay," Stephanie said. "Believe that." She returned the hug, then she pulled back slightly to look into Marian's eyes. "I love you, too." She saw Marian nod, a small smile flitting across her mouth, and she gave her a smile that disappeared almost as soon as it appeared.

"I assume the best thing to do if Helen's ex-husband calls is to tell him you're just a friend who's taking care of Katie and that you don't know how she got here. Which is true, of course. You don't know at this point what happened." When Marian nodded her agreement, she turned back to Helen, but as she turned, she caught sight of the casement window across the room.

Slowly, the closed window seemed to swing open. A glint of metal appeared at the edge of the frame. There was a bright flash of blinding light. With effort, she shut out the image and turned to Helen. "There's not much time. We have to—"

At that moment, the door to Katie's bedroom opened, and the little girl wandered into the hallway, rubbing her eyes. Helen took a step in her direction, but Marian put her hand on Helen's arm. "I'll get her," she said. She went to Katie, and as she picked her up, Katie looked down the hall toward the living room.

"Mommy?"

Marian smiled at her. "She's going out for just a minute, Katie. She'll be back in a little while. My name's Marian. I'm a friend of your Mommy's and Woody's, and I'm going to stay with you until your Mommy gets back, okay?"

"I suppose," Katie said slowly. She leaned farther to the side and looked around Marian. "Where's Woody?"

The telephone rang, and Marian heard the conversation between Stephanie and Helen come to an abrupt halt. She hesitated for a second and then took Katie into the bedroom. "Woody had to go somewhere, too, Katie." She stood Katie on the floor and sat down on the bed.

"She's going to be back," Katie said. It was a statement that required no answer.

Marian patted the bed. "Would you like to sit beside me? I'd like to hold you on my lap," she said, putting her hand on her stomach, "but I'm going to have a baby pretty soon, and I'm afraid it would be hard for you to sit here."

Katie looked at her inquisitively. "You're going to have a baby?" She made her way onto the bed and sat beside Marian.

Marian smiled at her. "Yep."

Katie stared at Marian's stomach for several seconds, then she looked up at her. "When's Woody coming back?"

"I'm not sure."

The little girl nodded and looked toward the door. "Well, she said we're all going to live together again." She paused and smiled up at Marian. "Forever."

"Well," Marian said, "forever's a really long time, and I can't think about forever right now when I'm so hungry. How about you? Would you like some breakfast?"

"Yep," Katie replied.

Marian put her arms around the little girl and, holding her, stood with some difficulty. She ignored a slight twinge in her abdomen. She had felt one last night, and it had gone away in seconds. "I don't know my way around here, Katie. Do you think you can show me where things are?"

Katie nodded. "Sure. Can I have anything I want to for breakfast?"

Marian looked at her carefully. "And what might that be?"

"Oh," Katie said, "maybe some cookies."

Marian raised an eyebrow. "Well, I think we might have to talk about that."

Katie sighed. "That's what Mommy says," she responded in obvious resignation.

Marian laughed softly and turned toward the door. She started when she saw Helen, ashen-faced, standing in the doorway.

"That was Doug," Helen said quietly. "He said he's had the police looking for Katie since yesterday morning. They're coming here now."

Marian looked past Helen to where Stephanie was standing in the hall, her face grim. When she saw Marian looking at her, she shook her head.

Marian gave Katie to Helen, who held her to her chest tightly, her eyes filling with tears.

"I love Woody," Helen said softly. "Tell her, if you can."

"Yes. Of course." Marian gave Helen's shoulder a sympathetic squeeze, then she went after Stephanie, who had gone back to the living room. Marian watched as Stephanie zipped up her windbreaker.

"Are you going now?"

Stephanie glanced at her. "I can't wait any longer. There's not much time."

"Okay." Marian picked up her own jacket and shrugged into it.

"What are you doing?"

"We're leaving, right?"

"You're not. You're staying here. You said you would."

"That was when I thought Helen was going with you. Helen's not going, so I am."

"Look—" Stephanie started.

"No," Marian said firmly, "you look this time. I'm damned well going with you, and I don't want to hear any more about it. If you leave without me, I'll take Helen's car. I'm sure she wouldn't mind. Also," she said, as Stephanie started to protest again, "I know the area down there better than you do. Corky dragged me down to the Municipal Market when you were seeing clients here last fall. It's close to the Capitol."

Stephanie opened her mouth to say something, then groaned and rubbed the heels of her hands at her eyes.

Marian frowned and took Stephanie's wrist. "What's wrong?"

Stephanie shook her head as if she were trying to shake off something. "It's okay."

"Right," Marian said derisively. "That's it. I don't want to hear any more arguments."

Stephanie sighed and nodded her head finally.

Marian opened the front door. "Do you want me to drive?"

"No. I'll be okay. Really."

Marian looked at her closely. "You'll let me know if it starts getting worse?" She waited for Stephanie's nod and then said, "Well, let's go." As she stepped into the hall, though, Stephanie touched her arm, and Marian turned to her.

Stephanie's voice held a note of pleading. "I really wish you wouldn't go. Something seems wrong. Are you sure you feel okay?"

Marian leaned forward and kissed her briefly. "I'm going to be fine, sweetheart," she said softly. "Now let's go. You said we don't have much time."

3

"Your notes, Governor."

Harold Donaldson waited, the notes in his hand. It seemed to him that the majority of his time was spent waiting. It had been obvious from the beginning of their relationship that Prestwood enjoyed making people wait.

Donaldson himself liked to move fast. The U.S congressman he had worked for before coming back home to Georgia had liked that about him. Here, in Prestwood's office, he had to rein in his natural quickness. A friend from New York had said it was because it was the Southern way. But that wasn't it, Donaldson knew. Prestwood's making his aide wait had to do with having control over people. It made him feel more powerful to know they were waiting for him.

"Put them on the desk."

Prestwood, who had been standing in front of the window in his office at the State Capitol, his back to Donaldson when he entered the room, turned but did not look at his aide. It was almost as if it were beneath him to do so unless he were making a point or had himself in just the proper frame of mind.

"Yes, sir." Donaldson placed the sheaf of notes on the corner of the huge desk. "Anything else you need before you leave, Governor?"

Prestwood picked   . "Looks
like a long speech." He   tempt at
a smile. The smile th   at of the
cameras or when he '   stituents
seemed most notable l

He had not, Donalds   stion. He
was making him wait again. A note of ......   t into his
voice. "Anything else, Governor?"

Prestwood looked up at him with just the slightest narrow-
ing of his eyes, obviously having heard the tone.

It was easy to see why he made such a superb politician,
Donaldson had often thought. Nothing really escaped Prestwood's notice, although he was very good at not showing it
when it was to his benefit. In a press conference, Donaldson had
observed, the man seemed to have tunnel vision, given the way
he ignored those members of the press who had offended him
in the past.

"No, Donaldson. Nothing else."

Donaldson turned to leave and had his hand on the doorknob when Prestwood spoke his name again. The tone was that
of a man who was concerned about something but didn't want
anyone to know. He turned. "Sir?"

"The threat that psychic from Florida was talking about.
What did you do about it?"

Donaldson gave a good imitation of a sincere frown. "You
told me not to do anything, Governor."

Prestwood smiled, but the corners of his mouth turned
down an almost imperceptible bit. "That's right. Just wanted to
make sure no one thinks I'm reacting to some psychic mumbo-
jumbo."

"No, sir," Donaldson replied. He left the office, and as he
was closing the door behind him, he smiled.

So the bastard was worried about it now, was he? So let him
worry. His aide was certainly not going to tell him he had
alerted the head of security, who was putting on more guards
today than was usual even for a gubernatorial appearance.
Since most of them would be in plain clothes, no one would

know unless it was necessary. If nothing happened, the governor would certainly never know. If something happened, though, Harold Donaldson's ass would be covered, because if Prestwood lived, it would be just like him to say he had told Donaldson to take care of the threat.

And Harold Donaldson was not about to be left out to twist in the wind if anything came down afterwards.

4

Stephanie turned the key in the ignition, and nothing happened. She frowned and turned the key again. Finally, on the third try, the engine caught minimally and coughed into life for a few seconds before it cut off again.

"Jesus H. Christ on a friggin' roller coaster." Marian groaned and shook her head. "I hate to say it, but I wish to hell we'd broken in and gotten my car."

Just then, the engine roared to life, billowing smoke from the exhaust pipes. Stephanie released the brake, put the car into first gear, and pulled into the street.

"Edgewood?" Marian asked.

"Yes. Helen said to go to Courtland and take a left. That should take us right by it."

Marian frowned. "I thought the street that goes by the Capitol was Washington."

Stephanie turned onto Edgewood and then glanced at Marian. "I don't know. I wasn't paying any attention to street names the other time."

"Me neither, but I assume it just changes names or something down there." She took a deep breath and released it. "Are we going to make it in time?"

"I think so," Stephanie said. But she knew they were going to face problems in the next minutes that were going to make the likelihood of their stopping Woody very slim. Not the least of which was the roaring in her head. It had started as she and Marian got into the car, and with each passing block, it seemed to grow louder. She had been having trouble identifying the noise at first, but now it was obvious.

It was the crowd roaring in her nightmare.

5

Mary Fowler looked out the window of the cab and had to crane her neck to see the dome from the street. A slight shiver of excitement ran through her, and she smiled at herself. She was so proud of George, it was hard to contain it sometimes.

When it became obvious that the driver was not going to get out, she opened the door herself, but as she was about to slide out, she looked back at George, puzzled. The driver had turned in the front seat to get paid, and George was making no move to pay him.

"What's wrong, George?" She looked at him more closely. His face was a pasty white, and sweat was beaded on his forehead. She leaned over to touch his cheek. "George. What's wrong?"

He shook his head and attempted a small smile. "Nothing. Just a little headache, I guess."

"A headache? That's ridiculous. You've never turned white and started sweating from a headache before."

The cab driver interrupted her. "Uh, lady, I got lots of fares I need to get. I don't want to hurry you, but—"

"Okay, okay," Mary muttered. "Honey, I think we should go get you a doctor. You don't look good at all."

He roused himself, took a handkerchief out of his pocket, and wiped his face. "No. That's okay. I'm feeling better now."

Mary frowned. Color was coming back into his face, but she didn't like the looks of this. "You're not having chest pains, are you? Tell me the truth."

George managed a slight smile. "No, no. Of course not. I told you, it's just a headache." He reached for his wallet and paid the driver, then slid out toward her.

As he stood, Mary took his arm. "This afternoon," she said, "we're taking you to a doctor. You've got a lot of pressure on you these days, and it's been a while since you had a checkup." His protest was met with firmness. "I told you, this afternoon. I won't listen to any excuses."

He shook his head. "Okay, okay," he said with resignation. "This afternoon."

6

"What's that?" Stephanie stared straight ahead down Edgewood Avenue, where traffic seemed to be backing up.

"God, I don't know," Marian said. She leaned to her right to get a better view. "It looks like an accident in front of the Municipal Market."

"Great," Stephanie muttered. "Do you know if there's any other street we can take?"

Marian thought for a minute and then shook her head. "Not any street that wouldn't take us way out of our way. We could go back to the street we just passed and cut over to Auburn Avenue, I think, but then we'd have to go through Five Points, and we can't turn there anywhere." She grimaced. "Besides, Corky was saying yesterday that there's been a lot of changes at Five Points. I might not be able to find my way around now."

"Maybe it's easier to get through now?"

Marian sighed. "I have no idea."

"Damn," Stephanie muttered, "I just remembered what intersection you're talking about." She heaved a huge sigh. "Well, I don't see that we've got any choice."

"Wait. Turn around. Go back to the interstate."

"We'll be going out of our way."

"Well, we'll be going out of our way to go through Five Points, too. It's probably going to be as fast to take the interstate from where we are now."

Stephanie nodded and reached for the gear shift. She backed up until the driver in the car behind her blew his horn anxiously, then she wrenched the wheel as far as it would go and made a U-turn. At the bridge where the interstate crossed Edgewood, she gunned the motor and cut in front of a car coming toward them in order to make the light.

Marian grabbed for the bar on the dashboard.

"Sorry," Stephanie said as she straightened the car.

Marian shook her head. "As long as you get us there in one piece, don't worry about me."

Stephanie gave her a half-smile. "That's what I like. A co-pilot with nerves of steel."

Marian laughed shortly. "Don't count on it. What I'm holding onto is called a chicken bar, remember."

7

Charles Becker shifted his feet so they were planted firmly and locked his hands behind his back in the parade-rest stance. He had assumed the stance so often in the Army that he now took it out of habit when he was standing guard. Eddie Jahnchek, the younger man standing opposite him at the door to the gallery, had been fidgeting the whole hour they had been there.

"You ain't been doing this long, have you, son?"

Jahnchek looked at him, and a trace of defensiveness crept into his voice. "Why do you say that?"

Becker grinned. "Because you been wiggling around like you got ants in your pants, boy. If you're gonna be doing this kind of work for long, you got to learn how to be still. The way you're fidgeting, you'll wear yourself out in a couple of hours. And besides that, if you're still, you see more. See, you're still, like a coiled spring sort of, and then when you need to, you can move — fast."

"Yeah, I suppose," Jahnchek said.

After a moment, Becker noticed that his partner had managed to slow his fidgeting a little, but ten minutes later, he was at it again. "Sheeit," Becker muttered under his breath. A movement in the hall caught his eye. A group of people was coming toward them. Soon, the place would be a madhouse.

Becker frowned. Among those in the first group was the girl with the trombone. He glanced toward Eddie. He hoped when he asked to look into her case, she didn't say anything about how he had let her pass before without looking. He shouldn't have done it anyway. It had been stupid.

When she came abreast of them, he smiled at her and reached for the case. Frowning, she pulled back a little.

"Sorry, Miss," he said. "We've got to check all packages and large cases. You understand." He flashed a look in Eddie's direction.

She followed the glance and then smiled at him. "Sure. I understand." She looked down the hall. "I don't need to go in yet, though. There's no point in getting it checked twice, right?"

When it became obvious that she was not going to hand over the case, he put his hand down by his side again and smiled in return. "No, Miss. We'll just wait until you're ready to go in."

As she started to leave, he touched the side of his index finger to his cap. It wouldn't hurt the kid to see a pro in action. He might pick up a few pointers that would help him later. He watched as she strode down the hall and turned into the women's restroom.

8

Woody pushed open the restroom door and made her way to the last stall. Inside, she set the case down on the floor and leaned back against the cool tiles. She closed her eyes and clenched her fists.

There was a scream in her gut, where the rage resided. It threatened to come up into her throat and be released, but she closed her mouth and refused to allow the sound to escape. She held it until her throat felt like it was closing up and she wouldn't be able to breathe. Finally, it slid back down, taking the burning bile with it.

She opened her eyes, took a deep breath, and let it out slowly, slowly. With the calming of her breathing, she felt she could think again. She had been stupid to believe that it was going to be easy. She sat down on the ledge that ran along the wall, closed her eyes again, and tried to think.

After a moment, her eyes flew open. The woman guard just outside the restroom was about her size. If she could get the uniform, she could get out of the restroom without that pig at the gallery door seeing her, and she could make her way down to the other gallery door. There were guards down there that she hadn't seen before.

She rubbed at her forehead. But what about the rifle? She tried to remember what the guy in the gun shop had said about the handguns in the case. Maybe the guns the guards carried could shoot that far. She took a deep breath and released it. They would have to. She didn't have any other choice. She'd worry about the capabilities of the gun after she got it.

She stood and started toward the door, but she stopped as she put her hand on the door handle. She'd have to hurt the guard to get the uniform, and the guard was a woman.

She put her hands to her head and groaned. It was getting so complicated. It had seemed easy before, when she was planning it. Now, she was thinking about hurting someone who might not even be part of that cancer she was trying to destroy.

The voice was talking softly to her.

She lifted her head. The woman was wearing a uniform. That meant she was trying to protect the cancer so that it could grow and get bigger, whether she knew it or not.

Woody put her hand on the handle again and opened the door.

9

Mabel Palmer stood on the staircase leading up to the second floor and rested for a minute. Her hip had been aching since she had gotten up this morning, and now there was a shooting pain in it that went all the way down through her left knee and into her ankle. "You're a crazy old woman, Mabel Palmer," she muttered under her breath. She could always take the elevator, but there was something about the pleasure of climbing the magnificent staircase that outweighed the pain.

Down below her, in the lobby, newspaper and television people milled around. She chuckled. It was easy to tell which ones were going to be in front of the camera; most of them seemed more concerned about their clothes than the story.

But there were others around today that she couldn't place. She frowned. There were the usual extra guards, because the governor was going to be talking, but these people were in street clothes. The look was the same, though — they were trying to look like everybody else who was there. Most of them were trying too hard.

As she looked at a young white man at the foot of the staircase, he glanced across the lobby. She turned to follow the direction of his gaze and saw a black man with short, salt-and-pepper hair nod to the one on the staircase.

They were like children playing at a game, she thought. But as that thought crossed her mind, she felt a prick of anxiety at the back of her mind. Something was wrong today. She felt it in the air.

"You really are getting to be an old lady, Mabel Palmer," she said. She took a deep breath, put her attention on the top of the stairs, and started climbing again, one step at a time, trying to ignore the pain. She was going to have to see that doctor again.

10

As Stephanie rounded a curve on the Downtown Connector, she spotted ahead the bridge that took the east-west interstate over the Connector. She took a deep breath. She definitely did not need her first glimpse of the Capitol to overwhelm her as it had the last time.

Seconds later, she left the shadow of the overpass and deliberately turned her head away from the direction of the Capitol. When she was sure she had passed the point where she could see the gold dome from the interstate, she turned her head back and found that she was too close to the exit ramp.

Wrenching the wheel sharply to the right, she put her arm out to brace Marian against the seat and jammed on the brakes. Halfway up the ramp, she glanced at her.

"Still okay?"

Marian rolled her eyes up. "Don't interrupt me while I'm praying, dear."

Stephanie gave her a fleeting smile, but as she looked back out the windshield, she spotted the Capitol out of the corner of her eye, and an explosion seemed to blow her head apart.

The car swerved as she put her hand up to her head. She barely had time to get the car off the ramp before another explosion ripped through her chest.

11

Mary Fowler adjusted her skirt and sat down. Turning, she smiled at the older black woman who was sitting next to her. "This is quite exciting, isn't it?"

The woman smiled in return. "Well," she said, "it's not going to be as exciting once they start talking."

Mary chuckled. "I suppose you're right." Looking down, she twisted her hands around the handle of her purse. She felt as proud as she had when her first girl had stood up and recited a poem at the PTA meeting years ago. She was so proud she just had to tell someone. She turned to the woman again.

"I don't mean to be bothering you, ma'am—"

The woman allowed another smile to cross her face. "Why, you're not bothering me. You give me just half a chance, and I'll talk your ear off."

"Well, it's silly," Mary said. "But I'm gonna bust wide open, if I don't tell somebody." She gestured toward the floor, where a beehive of activity was taking place. "My husband's one of the representatives. He was just appointed by the governor a few months ago, and this is the first chance I've had to come here and see him."

"Why, you don't say! Now isn't that something. Well, it's nice to know the wife of one of our representatives." She put her hand out. "My name's Mabel Palmer."

Mary took the woman's large, warm hand. "Mary Fowler. My husband's name is George. We're from Hardwick."

Mabel frowned slightly. "That'd be Erskine County?"

"That's right." Mary lifted her eyebrows. "To tell you the truth, I didn't know anybody in the big city had ever heard of Erskine."

Mabel chuckled. "My folks was — were farmers, ma'am. My daddy used to work some land down there. It sure was hard on us, I'll tell you." She smiled. "But we had each other, and that meant a lot."

"That's the most important, isn't it?" Mary said.

"I'd say so." Mabel frowned slightly. "But I do know how hard it was, and I know it's still hard down there, trying to earn a living from ground that's been worked too hard, too long."

"Well, my husband wants to do something about that, Mrs. Palmer."

"My name's Mabel," she said, putting her hand on Mary's.

"Then you must call me Mary."

Mabel smiled. "Well, Mary, would you show me your husband?"

Mary nodded her head, pleased. She leaned closer to the rail and spotted George, who was standing near the front, talking to another man. She pointed. "He's that one. There. He's stand-ing up talking to the man in the—" She chuckled as she noticed the man's tie. "The one in the flowered tie."

Mabel patted Mary's hand. "My, he's a good-looking man." She cocked her head to one side. "He's got a kind look some-how. My children would say I was being silly, but I can tell. He's a good man."

Mary nodded, a small smile crossing her face. "Yes," she said softly. "He is."

12

She kept hearing Marian's voice. It was coming from far away.

The motorcade had rounded the bend and was approaching Dealy Plaza. She tried to disentangle her feet from the dirty wooden floor so she could start the run toward the young man with the gun who stood so far to her right. As she looked into the street, the crowd roared more loudly. The boy waving the flag bounced up and down on his father's shoulders.

With as much effort as she could muster, she pulled herself back to the car and Marian's presence.

"Are you okay?" Marian's face was a picture of grave concern.

Stephanie did not quite manage a smile. She patted Marian's arm. "I'm fine. Don't worry." She took a deep breath and reached for the gear shift.

"The hell you are," Marian muttered. "Push your seat back and get out of the car. I'm driving."

The firm tone left no room for argument. Stephanie reached for the lever to push the seat back so Marian could fit under the wheel.

13

Chris Lowery, a security guard who had been called in on her regular day off, stood in the hallway near the women's restroom and watched as people stood in line to have their packages checked by the guards at the gallery door.

She took a deep breath and exhaled. What she wanted in the worst way right now was a cigarette. She had stopped three months ago, and most of the time she didn't even think about it any more. But once in a while, like now, the craving came over her so powerfully that she could hardly stand it.

She shifted from one foot to the other while she considered asking Charlie Becker. The man was a world-class asshole, but at least he smoked. The question was whether it was worth asking him. He'd been ragging her about quitting, and he purposefully blew smoke her way whenever she happened to be unlucky enough to be in the guard room at the same time. If she asked him for a smoke, she'd probably never hear the end of it.

She frowned as she watched the woman with the case go into the restroom. There was something strange about her. She'd been talking to Charlie as if she knew him, though, so maybe it was just paranoia. With practiced nonchalance honed by years of working with "the boys," as her roommate put it, she strolled over to the galley door. She smiled at the elderly man who was explaining to Charlie that he must have lost his pass.

"Charlie." She tapped him on the shoulder.

Becker leaned toward her without taking his eyes off the people in line. "Yeah, Lowery."

"You were talking to that woman with the case a minute ago."

"Yeah. What about it?"

"Have you seen her before?"

Becker looked at her and smirked. "Christ. You're getting as jumpy as Palmer. You bucking for a promotion or something?"

"What's that mean?"

"Well, he saw her one day with that case she carries, and he come running down the hall like somebody's givin' him the hot foot." He glanced at her. "It ain't a goddamn bomb, for God's sake," he whispered, "it's a fuckin' trombone."

"Have you looked today?"

Becker shook his head in disbelief. "You've been seeing too many Dirty Harry movies, Lowery." He cut his eyes back up the hall where she had come from. "Why don't you get back to your post, okay? Stop worrying."

She stiffened. "You don't need to tell me my job, Becker. You're not over me, you know."

Becker leaned closer and whispered in her ear. "No, but I'd like to be over you, darlin'."

Lowery's first inclination was to pull away, but she made herself immobile. It wasn't the first time Becker's conversations with her had contained sexual innuendoes, but for some reason, they always took her by surprise.

She gave him what she knew he would see as an intimate smile, then she murmured softly, "I'd rather swallow razor blades, Becker."

Without looking at his face, she turned and walked back down the hall. When she reached the spot she had been standing at before, she looked back. Becker's back was ramrod stiff. She grinned. She'd gotten to him with that one.

A moment later, the woman with the case opened the door. She looked ill. She had her hand to her forehead, and her voice was barely audible, but it was obvious the woman was talking to her. Lowery went to the door.

"Look, I feel like I'm going to faint. Could you help me a minute, please?" The woman took a deep breath and seemed to sway.

Lowery frowned, took the woman's elbow to support her, and moved her back into the restroom. "Do you know what's wrong?"

The woman shook her head. "No," she whispered. "It just came on very suddenly. I'm sick at my stomach, and I feel dizzy."

"Sounds like it could be the flu. We'll just sit here for a minute and see if you feel any better. If you don't, I'll have someone get you a doctor." She watched as the woman nodded slowly.

Carefully, Lowery helped her sit down on the ledge beside the window, and then she went to the sink and pulled a few paper towels from the dispenser. She wet them under running water from the faucet, and seconds later, she started to turn back, intending to hold the damp towels on the woman's forehead.

At that moment, though, she felt a crack on her head that became a massive explosion behind her eyes and sent her to her knees. As she tried to hold on to the sink, she felt her fingers slip, and then the blackness closed in.

14

"I think this next street's it," Marian said. She frowned and glanced at Stephanie. "Are you going to make it?"

Stephanie nodded. She had been sitting with her elbow propped on the passenger's window, holding her head. "I'll make it. It's getting better."

Marian shook her head and turned the car onto the street that would take them around to the right side of the Capitol from the back. She came down hard on the accelerator as she straightened the wheel and then saw the crossing guard standing in the middle of a crosswalk near Piedmont Avenue. She groaned and banged the heel of her hand against the steering wheel as she came to a stop.

The guard blew a whistle, and people from both sides of the street entered the yellow-striped area. Just as the street was almost clear again, a young woman wearing a backpack and carrying a sheet of paper stopped beside the guard. She pointed to the paper and then to the building across the street. The guard smiled and turned his back to the line of traffic that was beginning to form behind the VW. Marian tooted the horn, and he looked back. As Marian started to pull forward, he motioned for her to stay at the line, and she muttered an obscenity under her breath.

"We've got no time," Stephanie said. Her voice was raspy.

Marian tooted the horn again, and when the guard looked up, his face showing irritation, she gunned the engine and took off, leaving him blowing his whistle at her.

Moments later, she pulled up in front of the huge, columned building and turned to Stephanie. Her face was white, and she was staring into space. Marian put her hand on Stephanie's arm.

"Sweetheart?"

Stephanie closed her eyes briefly, and when she opened them again, she gave Marian a small smile. "I'm okay." But as her attention was drawn to the massive doors of the building, she frowned.

"There's no one here."

"What?"

Stephanie waved her hand toward the sidewalks and wide steps leading up to the doors. Her voice took on a note of intensity. "Nobody's *out* here. What time—" She looked down at her watch and groaned. "It's later than I thought. Why don't you find somewhere to park the car and then—"

"Let's leave the car here. I doubt seriously that I can find a parking place."

Stephanie shook her head. "We'll get towed." She reached for the door handle. "Drive around the block or something. I don't want you inside anyway."

"Forget it," Marian said grimly.

"What if they tow the car while it's here?"

"From your mouth to God's ear."

"Look," Stephanie started, but the pounding had begun again, and it seemed to take all of her energy just to keep her head from exploding. She pressed the heel of her hand to her temple.

"We'll get the car later if they tow it," Marian said firmly. "Let's just get going." As she saw Stephanie nod her head, she jerked the keys out of the ignition and began to slide out from under the steering wheel. Just then, she felt another sharp pain stab through her abdomen, and she gasped softly. She glanced over to see if Stephanie had noticed, but Stephanie was coming around the back of the car. She stood up, and the pain seemed to be gone. Marian shut the car door and hurried to catch up with Stephanie.

15

Woody opened the restroom door just a crack and peered up the hall toward the gallery door where the guard she knew as

Becker stood. His back was to her, as before; the younger one was stifling a yawn as he turned to look down the hall behind him.

As she stepped into the hall, she adjusted the holstered weapon she carried now on her right hip. The uniform was an almost perfect fit.

16

Stephanie pounded up the broad front steps of the Capitol with Marian behind her. At the top of the steps, she stopped for a moment, her hand on the door. "You don't have any idea where the gallery is, do you?"

Marian shook her head. "No. I've never been inside before."

Stephanie grimaced and opened the door. There was no guard at the stand inside, obviously where passes were issued. She glanced across the lobby and caught the eye of a heavyset woman in a security guard's uniform.

The guard, who was leaning over a desk in a corner of the lobby, talking to a man in a business suit, straightened. "Be with you in a minute," she called, then she turned back to the conversation.

Stephanie shoved her hands into her pockets and fidgeted while the conversation went on. After a moment, though, she took her hands out of her pockets and surreptitiously slid one hand across the top of the stand, where several clip-on passes lay. She palmed two of them, handed one to Marian, and clipped one onto her belt, then stepped to the side of the stand. She pointed to the plastic-enclosed pass and smiled.

"That's okay," she called to the guard, "we still have our passes. We were just out for a minute."

The guard frowned slightly.

"Has the governor started his address yet?" Stephanie smiled even more broadly.

Finally, the guard smiled back at her. "He just went up. You might not miss more than a minute or two of it."

Stephanie nodded and walked purposefully toward the crossing hallway at the back of the lobby, trying to keep herself from running. When she reached it, she closed her eyes briefly and tried to push aside the images that flooded her mind again.

The motorcade drew closer. The flags on either side of a sleek, shining hood snapped and popped in the breeze.

The young man to her right was lifting the rifle to the window.

"No," she whispered. With effort, she shut out the images and concentrated on the present. She felt a strong mental tug to her right, and she opened her eyes and grabbed at Marian's arm. "This way," she said.

She was almost halfway up the stairs leading to the next floor, however, when she heard Marian's voice behind her. Turning back, she saw Marian leaning against the marble railing at the foot of the stairs, holding her stomach. Fear blossomed in the middle of her chest, and she took the stairs down two steps at a time.

"Marian? What's wrong?"

Marian gave her a shaky half-smile. "I don't know. I just felt a sharp pain when I got out of the car, and it went away. It was worse for just a second." She took a deep breath, released it, and gave Stephanie a more confident smile. "It's gone now. Really. It's nothing to worry about, dear."

She put her hand on the railing and took one step before Stephanie stopped her.

17

Jerry Kaplan put his hands up to rub his eyes. They felt gritty from a lack of sleep. Tomorrow morning, he thought, he was going to start checking the want ads. Whether he wanted to admit it or not, Judy was right. Working as a security guard had paid enough when there were just the two of them, but now that they had three kids, he had to work two jobs just to make ends meet. It was the night job at the Equitable Building that was killing him. He never seemed to get enough sleep.

He yawned and noticed that a guard who had entered the gallery a few minutes ago was still standing at the back wall, her arms folded over her chest, apparently watching the activity on the House floor.

He frowned slightly. Something was not quite right, but he wasn't sure what it was. He didn't recognize her, but that was nothing strange. There were a lot of new guards lately. No, it was something about the way she looked.

He spotted what was wrong and smiled. When he had a chance, he was going to have to tell the new kid on the block that the standard uniform did not include white sneakers.

18

Governor Robert Prestwood sat on the platform near the podium and watched the flurry of activity around him on the floor of the House. He crossed his right leg over his left knee and then remembered what a friend had once said about Nixon crossing his legs that way.

"The jackass had his legs crossed so tightly that he looked like he couldn't possibly have any balls."

Prestwood's brow furrowed ever so slightly. He was going to have to ask his image man about that. Maybe putting his ankle on his knee would be considered more masculine, although he knew other politicians who crossed their legs the way he did. He was still mulling over the matter when the Speaker pro tem leaned down to ask him if he would be ready in a moment.

Prestwood did not look at him, but he made sure the man heard the frost in his voice. "I've been ready for ten minutes now."

When the man moved away, Prestwood looked up toward the gallery and smiled. It never hurt to smile at his constituents. Most of them, he firmly believed, cast their ballots based on smiles and bullshit rather than the issues, anyway. He'd smile now and give them the bullshit later.

He glanced down at the speech cards he was holding on his thigh and smiled inwardly. Next time, Donaldson was going to have to give him the bullshit sooner so he could rehearse it better before he gave it to the people.

But following upon that line of thought was a distinctly unpleasant one. Donaldson had seemed truly concerned about the problem with that psychic from Florida. Suppose she were right? This would be a perfect time for someone to get at him if they wanted to. He felt a slight sinking of his stomach.

He glanced up at the gallery again and scanned the rows packed with people. As he looked, his stomach readjusted itself to a normal position. There were not only the usual guards at each of the entrances into the gallery, but there had been one standing at the back who was now making her way toward the railing, obviously vigilant as she moved down the aisle steps. She seemed to be observing each and every person near the front of the gallery.

His thoughts were interrupted again as he heard the Speaker of the House introduce him, and Prestwood smiled broadly at the applause as he stood and crossed to stand at the podium.

19

Stephanie raced up the stairs, her heart pounding so loudly she could hear it. As she rounded a curve in the marble railing, she glanced two floors below to see the woman security guard from the lobby put her arm around Marian's waist.

She clenched her fist and slammed it down on the railing as she hesitated. Maybe she shouldn't have left her.

Go, Marian had said. *Stop her. Don't think about me. I'll be okay.* Then, gently, Marian had pushed her away. *Go, Stef. Now.* She began running again.

On the fourth floor, Stephanie paused at a corner to catch her breath. Her legs were trembling, she felt as if her lungs were on fire, and the stitch in her side was getting worse. She groaned, put her hand on her ribcage, and tried to breathe without coughing violently.

The crowd's roar was deafening in her ears.

When she could manage it, she straightened, looked up the hall, and saw what was apparently the gallery, a guard posted in front of its doors. She forced away the image of the young man with the rifle and got her legs moving again.

As she reached the doors, the guard put out a hand to stop her. She ripped the pass off her belt and pushed it at him, then she pulled open the door and groaned with dismay.

The gallery was packed, and it seemed that every person in it was standing, applauding. It was impossible to see anyone who might have a seat in the front row. Stepping inside, she began making her way along the back wall toward the aisle closest to her.

The guard was calling to her. She turned and saw that he was holding out her pass. She shook her head at him, and she thought for a moment that he was going to follow her, but he glanced toward the hallway and turned to go back outside.

As she reached the head of the aisle closest to her, people stopped applauding and started taking their seats. She looked down at the House floor and watched as the governor of Georgia stood at the podium on the floor below, waved his hand, and smiled broadly.

Her gaze swept the gallery, where people were settling themselves in their seats. She wiped perspiration off her forehead with the back of her hand and tried to slow her breathing. It was only then that she realized the images had vanished. Abruptly, the roaring in her ears was gone.

But the fear was still there. It was playing in her chest, tightening her muscles. The silence seemed to press against her. The danger was so thick in the air, she could scarcely breathe.

At that moment, Stephanie saw the guard standing next to the railing in front of the first row of seats. She felt a strange sensation at the back of her neck, as though her skin were crawling. The sensation spread and crept over her scalp. An involuntary sound started at the base of her throat, and she pushed it down, held it down as long as she could, but the fear forced it up her throat, and the sound came out as a small whimper.

The guard was the woman she had seen at the party.

It was Woody.

She had her hand on the butt of the pistol that hung at her waist. She was unsnapping the strap that held the pistol in the holster.

Gathering all of her mental energy, Stephanie went out to Woody's mind, but she knew even as she sent the thought that it would probably be sensed as no more than a whisper among all the other voices that were playing in Woody's head.

Woody.

Stephanie saw her hesitate for a moment, her hand still on the butt of the pistol, before she turned. She looked as if she were searching for something across an impossibly long distance. Then Stephanie saw her eyes, and the look of agony in them was like a knife plunging into Stephanie's chest, as if they were calling forth every feeling of pain she herself had ever experienced in her lifetime.

The brief instant seemed to last forever.

She was five years old, and her sister, her face twisted with the terrors of an uncontrollable mental power, rushed forward with a knife upheld in her hand. Reliving the horror of the moment, Stephanie cringed as the knife left its line of fire on her face again, felt the sickening drop of her stomach when she pushed against her sister's mind to stop the assault, saw her sister crouched in the corner of the white, bare room in the mental hospital, felt her mother's pain as clearly as she had the first time. She thought she might double over with the sudden agony that flooded her body, felt she might not live through that heartbreak again.

And she knew then that she would never be able to enter Woody's mind to stop her. It was only with effort that she remained on her feet.

A woman in the row closest to Stephanie glanced at her and leaned over to whisper something to her husband. He spoke to her, and she shrugged and turned her attention back to the House floor.

Stephanie shook her head slowly, and her eyes pleaded with Woody. She was so far away. So impossibly far away now.

Woody. No. Please.

She stopped a scream in her throat and began moving along in back of the last row again as Woody turned away and started pulling the pistol from the holster.

Just then, Stephanie's eye was caught by something that was happening on the House floor. She frowned, and her attention became riveted on the podium.

The governor was pushing to the side a stack of papers that had been on the podium. The top sheet was loose. It was starting to slip off the stack.

The slow-motion nightmare began.

The sheet of paper drifted toward the floor, down, down, floating on an invisible, insidious current of air.

With horrifying slowness, Stephanie turned toward Woody, who was still too far away, who was bringing the pistol up in her right hand, who was reaching with her left hand to steady it.

NO, Stephanie screamed, but it was a silent scream again, as if she had no voice powerful enough to utter the pain that filled her chest.

The governor's gaze followed the piece of paper as it floated to the floor.

Then Stephanie saw another man come forward from a seat near the podium, his feet moving as if they were mired in quicksand. As he neared the paper, he stretched out his hand and began to bend toward the floor.

It was the man she had seen in her dream.

It was the man she had seen with his arm around the boy's shoulders.

It was the man she had seen with Marian.

In a brief and terrible moment that seemed to stretch into eternity, she saw the woman this man loved standing beside him, and she saw the path they would walk in the years before them. She saw the juncture of that path where Marian waited with a small boy, and there was absolutely no doubt in her mind that the boy was the son that Marian was about to bring into the world.

But as she watched, the ground beneath their feet began to crumble, began to slide away into a gaping maw that had opened in the earth. She opened her mouth to scream, and the man turned toward her, frowning in puzzlement. Then he turned again and saw Marian and the boy. Bending, he grasped their outstretched hands as they fell from sight. A moment later, he had pulled them back and set them on solid ground.

The instant shimmered and disappeared. She turned back to Woody, her heart full of horror.

Woody had leveled the gun at the governor, her hands shaking, and a woman screamed from the second row of gallery seats. The governor's head came up, and he stared, mouth open, toward the gallery.

The man in Stephanie's dream had been standing just below the podium, smiling, his big hand outreached with the fallen piece of paper in it. When he heard the woman's scream and saw the governor's face, he turned his eyes toward the gallery, his smile fading.

Stephanie knew she was too far away.

She was always too far away.

She struggled to untangle her feet from the floor, strained to reach Woody in time, to stop the gun from firing just this one time. She heard the screams around her, saw people move away in that terrifying slowness to get out of danger. But just as she thought maybe she had a chance, just as she thought maybe, impossibly, Woody was not going to fire the pistol, she heard the explosion.

A sound started way down deep inside of her, gathered power, and was pushed out with so much force that she thought her throat might be torn. She cried out to Woody as she saw the man thrown backwards against the podium.

A wound in the side of George Fowler's head sprayed blood across the governor's crisp, white shirt. His body fell heavily in the silence that followed, and then Mary Fowler screamed out her husband's name.

Stephanie turned back to Woody. She was standing alone, the gallery seats empty all around her, the gun still smoking from the shot.

Woody turned and looked at Stephanie. After a moment, she dropped her eyes to the gun in her hands, and then she lifted them again.

A tear trickled down her cheek.

With deliberate slowness, she turned the pistol toward herself.

But as her finger curled around the trigger once more, Ezrah Palmer launched himself at her from the aisle.

EPILOGUE

1

Stephanie mayonnaised a piece of whole-wheat bread, laid a few lettuce leaves across it, and then plopped a slice of bologna in the middle. She folded the bread over and was bringing the half-sandwich to her mouth when the phone rang. Sighing, she put it down and leaned over the counter to answer the telephone.

"Stephanie?"

"Mmm."

"Corky."

Stephanie smiled. "I was just going to call you. I've got some good news for Helen."

"Well, I think she needs it. Helen saw Woody yesterday. She still won't talk to her. Helen seems to think she's never going to come back."

"But she is going to," Stephanie said. "Maybe not tomorrow or even the day after—the healing's going to take some time. Maybe a lot of time. But one day, she'll be back."

"Well, I'm having some trouble convincing Helen of that. She told me this morning that she was watching a program on PBS last night about schizophrenia. 'The Violent Mind.' I don't think it was very comforting."

"No. I don't imagine it was." Stephanie picked up the sandwich and went to sit at the kitchen table. "But a lot of schizophrenics don't respond well to counseling or medication. Woody's not one of them. She's—lost right now. It's going to take a while to get back. But she is going to get back."

"Your word on that?"

Stephanie smiled slightly. "Let's say I've got a very good feeling about it."

Corky chuckled. "I'll tell Helen." She paused. "At least she's got her friends while Woody's gone. She was saying a few weeks ago that she and Woody forgot that for a while. Through the trial and even afterwards, all of us were around, but when things started getting weird for them—I guess when Woody started going off the deep end—they shut themselves off from everybody." Corky's grin was almost audible. "I don't think Helen has a spare minute to herself now. Somebody's always dragging her off somewhere. I know it was hard at first. People they hadn't seen for a while would come up and ask about Woody, and she had to go over the whole thing again. But it seems to be getting easier. Every once in a while, she even enjoys herself for a few minutes. Sam and I took her to the Azalea Dance two weeks ago. Maybe you and Marian can make it next year."

"What is it?"

"The Azalea Dance! It's fantastic. The dyke event of the year, in my opinion. Wall-to-wall women, old-fashioned dance cards, dykes in party dresses and tuxes—or jeans— whatever you like. Party decorations. The works. Like prom night."

Stephanie laughed. "It sounds like fun. You'll probably have to remind us of it, though."

"Okay. By the way, am I talking too much? Sam says I get wound up sometimes and just keep rattling on for hours."

Stephanie smiled and shook her head. "No. It's good to know what's going on." She eyed the sandwich and reached for it.

"Well, my biggest thing with Helen right now is that she's still blaming herself. She says if she hadn't refused to cooperate with you, then maybe Woody wouldn't be where she is right now. That maybe none of this would've happened."

Stephanie frowned and placed the sandwich back on the paper towel. "Look, if it matters to Helen what I think about it, tell her that I don't know that it could have happened any differently, no matter what she did. All I know is that it happened the way it did. Maybe it was impossible for it to happen any other way."

"That's what Marian said."

"She did, did she? Was that her practical, everyday, walking-around self you were talking to?"

"What?"

Stephanie smiled again. "Nothing, Corky. When did you talk to her?"

"This morning. By the way, I got so wrapped up in telling you what was going on here that I forgot you said you had some good news."

"I talked to George Fowler this morning."

"The newspaper said he's going to be all right. Is that true?"

"Yes," Stephanie said. "He's going to be fine."

"And the security guard that Woody hit?"

"She was back at work a couple of days later. Luckily, it wasn't too serious, and she decided not to file charges."

"You think she's a sister?"

"What makes you think that?"

"I saw a picture of her in the paper. She looks like a dyke. It's probably just wishful thinking. It used to be you could tell. Now, even straight women look like dykes. If we had worn the kind of clothes ten years ago that they do now — jackets and fucking ties, for Christ's sake—they would've run us out of town on a rail."

Stephanie grinned, "I've had the same thoughts myself."

"So, anyway, I interrupted you again. The good news?"

"I think Fowler may be willing to help Woody."

"Woody almost killed the man, Stephanie. Why in hell would he help her?"

"Well, I guess you could say he's one of the good guys." She smiled. "With a little help from his wife, I suspect. They were both very understanding when they found out more about Woody. And about Helen and Katie. He said when Woody is released from treatment, he'll see that no charges are brought against her. He thinks he can handle the governor. I've got a feeling he can."

"Well, that is good news. I'll tell Helen when I talk to her again."

Stephanie hesitated a moment, and then she said quietly, "By the way, you can tell Helen that I think Katie's also going to be with her again."

"You're kidding."

"No. I wasn't going to say anything, but for the past couple of weeks, I've been seeing them together. The three of them. I think it must be time to tell Helen. Maybe," she said dryly, "if you tell her, then I can stop spacing out in the middle of the afternoon to watch this idyllic vision."

"I'll tell her. By the way, friend, I've got a message for you from Marian."

Stephanie lifted an eyebrow. "I was just going to see her. What's the message?" She reached for the sandwich again and took a bite, her hunger finally getting the best of her.

"She said," Corky responded, "that you should go to the Lighthouse to eat instead of fixing yourself bologna sandwiches."

Stephanie barely had time to swallow before she started laughing.

2

Stephanie pushed open the door to Marian's hospital room and looked in. Marian was sitting up, her gown open, the baby nursing at her breast.

"Every time I come to see you," Stephanie grinned, "he's having dinner. So to speak."

"Jealous?" Marian looked down and smiled. "Actually, I'm teaching him early that food is the most important thing in the world." She held her hand out to Stephanie. "Come here, sweetheart."

Closing the door, Stephanie went to stand close to the bed. She leaned over and kissed Marian and then drew up a chair. Smiling at the dark-haired infant, she laid her finger in the tiny palm. The hand closed around her finger in a tight fist.

"Hey, he's pretty strong." She wiggled her finger, and the baby's hand continued to clench it. His eyes rolled around to stare at her for a minute, and he moved his head so Marian's breast popped free from his mouth. Marian pulled the gown loosely over herself.

"Hey, he's smiling at me," Stephanie said.

"I can't believe you think that."

"You're not going to tell me that's gas?"

Marian shook her head in mock disbelief and reached for Stephanie's hand. "I can't wait to get home. I miss you so much."

"Me, too," Stephanie whispered.

"I expected Cat to keep you company. Isn't she doing a good job?"

"Well, she's sleeping on my head now instead of yours, if that's what you mean. She misses you, too. She just sits there sometimes and stares at me. I'm afraid I don't give her the same amount of attention you do."

"Well, tell her I'll be home tomorrow."

"Tomorrow?" Stephanie's eyes lighted up. "That's wonderful."

"Yes," Marian sighed. "It is. Did you get Mrs. Jacobs to agree to sit for him?"

"As soon as the fall semester starts, she'll sit with him in the afternoons while you're in class and I'm doing readings."

"Great." Marian pushed a thick lock of hair off the baby's forehead. "By the way, the nurse asked me this morning for the information on the birth certificate. His name and all." She paused for a moment and then looked at Stephanie. "I told her his name is Stephen Nowland Damiano."

Stephanie glanced at her with both surprise and pleasure apparent on her face. "I wasn't aware you were going to give him my name as his middle name."

Marian shrugged. "I wanted to do that. You don't mind, I take it?"

"Mind?" Stephanie grinned. "Of course I don't mind." She gently shook the baby's fist with her finger still clenched in it. "Stephen Nowland Damiano," she repeated softly. "I like that." She looked at Marian and held her eyes for a long moment. "I'll feel more like he's mine, too."

"Well, dear, speaking of that—" Marian took Stephanie's other hand and squeezed it. "I did something else I didn't ask you about."

"Oh?"

Marian chuckled softly. "I told the nurse his father's name was S.J. Nowland."

"My initials?" Stephanie gave her a questioning look. "My name?"

"That did occur to me," Marian said dryly. "She said she wanted the full name, but I told her that was the full name. She looked at me a little strangely. Then she said, 'Nowland. That's your friend's name, isn't it?' I said it was, indeed, my partner's name." Marian laughed out loud. "I think she thinks it must be your brother or something, and I don't think she understood what I meant by the word 'partner.' But, after all, she just puts down the information that the mother gives her."

Stephanie shook her head slowly, a grin starting to spread across her mouth. "You're something, you know that?"

Marian nodded. "I know." She sobered after a minute and looked down at the baby. Her voice was soft. "It's going to be all right, isn't it, Stef? I mean, we did the right thing, didn't we?"

Stephanie smiled gently. "Yes," she murmured. She brought Marian's hand up and kissed it. "You know we did."

They passed the next several minutes in silence before Stephanie spoke again.

"By the way, I ran into the Madam this morning."

"And is the Madam doing well these days?"

"She is." Stephanie sighed and leaned back in the chair. "She did an impromptu reading for me."

Marian chuckled. "Remember that cartoon we saw? Two psychics meet on the street, and one says to the other, 'So, how am I doing today?'"

Stephanie's smile was fleeting. "I didn't really want to, but I found myself telling her that I'm not sure I want to take on any more of these cases."

Marian groaned in sympathy. "My God, that must have set her off. She doesn't need any encouragement."

"I know."

After a lengthy silence, Marian gave Stephanie's hand a squeeze. "So what did she say?"

"She said I have to keep doing what I'm doing."

"Have to?"

"Mmm. She said that when a person has a gift, she's obligated to use it."

"Well, in the first place, you'd be using it by seeing your regular clients. In the second place, I'm not sure what she says is true. What if using that gift is harmful to you?"

"I don't know that it is."

Marian snorted.

"What's that supposed to mean?"

"Well, gee, I don't know. I don't suppose you've noticed that when you're trying to find missing people or chasing murderers that you don't sleep worth a damn, you don't eat right—not that you do anyway, but—"

"Maybe it just means that I haven't found a way to deal with it yet."

"Maybe." Marian squeezed Stephanie's hand again. "Look, with your regular clients, you can pull aside the curtain to let them in and then close it again. But with the other cases, especially when violence is involved—you don't have time to prepare yourself. It comes at you so forcefully that you can't close yourself off even when you need to. The question is, can you find some way to do that? Because if you feel you want to do this kind of work, you have to learn how to do it without it making you sick."

Stephanie heaved a sigh. "Maybe I can't. Maybe I just have to live with it." She paused. "I just hate that you have to live with it."

"Well, I'm not worried about—"

There was a knock, and before they had a chance to acknowledge it, the door opened. A young nurse stood in the doorway, looking at Stephanie.

"I'm sorry to bother you, but—" She nodded toward the hall. "I asked the nurse on duty to tell me when you got here."

"You wanted to see me?"

The nurse nodded, and her face twisted as if she were going to cry. "It's my brother. We haven't heard from him in three weeks now." Tears started, and she reached into the pocket of her uniform for a handkerchief. "Do you think you could help me?"

Stephanie turned to look at Marian, and her eyes held the sadness that Marian had seen many times before, but there was also a plea for understanding.

Marian patted Stephanie's hand. "Go on, sweetheart," she said. "After all, maybe it is our destiny."

Relief was evident in Stephanie's eyes. She leaned over and kissed Marian tenderly on the forehead. "Maybe so," she whispered. She straightened and took Marian's hand. "I guess as long as you're with me, I can deal with that. She searched Marian's eyes for a moment. "You?"

"Always," Marian said softly. She looked at the baby in her arms, and when she looked back up at Stephanie, a smile crinkled the corners of her deep, sea green eyes. "Have you ever really had any doubts about that?"

Stephanie returned the smile and shook her head. "No," she whispered. "No doubts at all."

Other books of interest from
ALYSON PUBLICATIONS

THE CRYSTAL CURTAIN, by Sandy Bayer, $8.00. Even as a child, Stephanie Nowland knew her psychic powers set her apart. Now an escaped murderer — a man she helped capture — is seeking revenge. Visions of her death and her lover's death fill his thoughts. Stephanie can see them, too. Will her powers, along with the support of the woman she loves, be enough to save them both?

BUSHFIRE, edited by Karen Barber, $9.00. Amidst many differences, all lesbians share one thing: a desire for women. Sometimes intensely sexual, other times subtly romantic, this emotion is always powerful. These short stories celebrate lesbian desire in all its forms. The authors portray a lazy affair set against the backdrop of Venice; a small-town stone butch being "flipped" by a stranger with painted fingernails; an intense but destructive relationship between a reporter and a mysterious dancer; and a holy encounter between a birthday girl, a call girl, and her rosary beads.

WHAT I LOVE ABOUT LESBIAN POLITICS IS ARGUING WITH PEOPLE I AGREE WITH, by Kris Kovick, $8.00. The truth is funnier than fiction. Here's an inside look at the wry and occasionally warped mind of Kris Kovick, featuring some 140 of her cartoons, plus essays on religion and therapy ("I try to keep them separate, but it's hard"), lesbians and gay men, politics, sexuality, parenting, and American culture.

OIL AND GASOLINE, by Billi Gordon and Taylor-Anne Wentworth, $8.00. With an honesty usually found only in small children or cameras, the authors of this heavily autobiographical novel grapple with their experiences with incest, dependency, child abuse, and the human will to survive. Their story is one of healing and power: the healing that can come only from forgiveness; the power that can come only from love.

LEAVE A LIGHT ON FOR ME, by Jean Swallow, $10.00. Morgan is a computer instructor who doesn't understand what exactly has happened to her long-term relationship with Georgia, or what exactly is happening to the rest of her when she stands near Elizabeth. Georgia, forced into exile from the South she loves and from the alcoholic family she both loves and hates, doesn't understand why, after six years of recovery, she still hasn't found her way home. And Elizabeth, the rich and beautiful doctor, doesn't understand why she can't keep a girlfriend. But Bernice, who watches and waits, understands a lot by just being herself. Together, they move from a difficult past into a passionate and hopeful future.

HEATHER HAS TWO MOMMIES, by Lesléa Newman, illustrated by Diana Souza, $8.00. As the daughter of a lesbian couple, three-year-old Heather sees nothing unusual in having two mommies. When she joins a playgroup and discovers that other children have "daddies," her confusion is dispelled by an adult instructor and the other children who describe their own different families. Warmly illustrated by Diana Souza, *Heather Has Two Mommies* realistically approaches issues central to lesbian parenting: artificial insemination, the birthing process, and the needs of a lesbian household.

GLORIA GOES TO GAY PRIDE, by Lesléa Newman; illustrated by Russell Crocker, $8.00. Gay Pride Day is fun for Gloria, and for her two mothers. Here, the author of *Heather Has Two Mommies* describes, from the viewpoint of a young girl, just what makes up this special day. Ages 3–7.

THE ADVOCATE ADVISER, by Pat Califia, $9.00. The Miss Manners of gay culture tackles subjects ranging from the ethics of zoophilia to the etiquette of a holy union ceremony. Along the way she covers interracial relationships, in-law problems, and gay parenting. No other gay columnist so successfully combines useful advice, an unorthodox perspective, and a wicked sense of humor.

CHOICES, by Nancy Toder, $9.00. Lesbian love can bring joy and passion; it can also bring conflicts. In this straightforward, sensitive novel, Nancy Toder conveys the fear and confusion of a woman coming to terms with her sexual and emotional attraction to other women.

DYKESCAPES, edited by Tina Portillo, $9.00. This anthology of lesbian short stories includes works by both new and established writers. Seventeen storytellers explore such diverse themes as racism, death, lesbian parenting, prison relationships, and interracial love and sex. They don't flinch from controversy: their stories also deal with role-playing, fat-positivity, and intergenerational affairs.

HAPPY ENDINGS ARE ALL ALIKE, by Sandra Scoppettone, $7.00. It was their last summer before college, and Jaret and Peggy were in love. But as Jaret said, "It always seems as if when something great happens, then something lousy happens soon after." Soon her worst fears turned into brute reality.

BI ANY OTHER NAME, edited by Loraine Hutchins and Lani Kaahumanu, $12.00. Hear the voices of over seventy women and men from all walks of life describe their lives as bisexuals. They tell their stories — personal, political, spiritual, historical — in prose, poetry, art, and essays. These are individuals who have fought prejudice from both the gay and straight communities and who have begun only recently to share their experiences. This ground-breaking anthology is an important step in the process of forming a community of their own.

THE ALYSON ALMANAC, $9.00. How did your representatives in Congress vote on gay issues? What are the best gay and lesbian books, movies, and plays? When was the first gay and lesbian march on Washington? With what king did Julius Caesar have a sexual relationship? You'll find all this, and more, in this unique and entertaining reference work.

CRUSH, by Jane Futcher, $8.00. It wasn't easy fitting in at an exclusive girls' school like Huntington Hill. But in her senior year, Jinx finally felt as if she belonged. Lexie — beautiful, popular Lexie — wanted her for a friend. Jinx knew she had a big crush on Lexie, and she knew she had to do something to make it go away. But Lexie had other plans. And Lexie always got her way.

BETWEEN FRIENDS, by Gillian E. Hanscombe, $8.00. The four women in this book represent radically different political outlooks and sexualities, yet they are tied together by the bonds of friendship. Through their experiences, recorded in a series of letters, Hanscombe deftly portrays the close relationship between political beliefs and everyday lives.

LAVENDER LISTS, by Lynne Y. Fletcher and Adrien Saks, $9.00. This all-new collection of lists captures many entertaining, informative, and little-known aspects of gay and lesbian lore: 5 planned gay communities that never happened, 10 lesbian nuns, 15 cases of censorship where no sex was involved, 10 out-of-the-closet law enforcement officers, and much more.

LESBIAN LISTS, by Dell Richards, $9.00. Lesbian holy days is just one of the hundreds of lists of clever and enlightening lesbian trivia compiled by columnist Dell Richards. Fun facts like uppity women who were called lesbians (but probably weren't), banned lesbian books, lesbians who've passed as men, herbal aphrodisiacs, black lesbian entertainers, and switch-hitters are sure to amuse and make *Lesbian Lists* a great gift.

DANCER DAWKINS AND THE CALIFORNIA KID, by Willyce Kim, $6.00. Dancer Dawkins views life best from behind a pile of hotcakes. But her lover, Jessica Riggins, has fallen into the clutches of Fatin Satin Aspin, the insidious leader of Violia Vincente's Venerable Brigade, and something has to be done about it. Meanwhile, Little Willie Gutherie of Bangor, Maine, renames herself the California Kid, stocks up on Rubbles Dubble bubble gum and her father's best Havana cigars, and heads west. When this crew collides in San Francisco, what can be expected? Just about anything...

DEAD HEAT, by Willyce Kim, $7.00. Willyce Kim's *Dancer Dawkins and the California Kid* delighted readers with a family of far-out characters. In *Dead Heat,* they meet again for a new adventure. While Dancer is trying to recover from her breakup with Jessica, the Kid has fallen for a gangster's girlfriend. Things get sticky when horse racing and a kidnapped Hungarian Viszla enter the picture, and the conclusion to the story is a day at the races you'll never forget.

LAVENDER COUCH, by Marny Hall, $8.00. What can you realistically expect to accomplish by seeing a therapist? How can you choose a therapist who's right for you? What should you consider when discussing fees? When is it time to get out of therapy? These are a few of the questions addressed here, in the first book that specifically addresses the concerns of gay men and lesbians who are considering therapy. Dr. Hall's advice will be invaluable for both individuals already in therapy, and those who are contemplating it.

LEGENDE, by Jeannine Allard, $6.00. Jeannine Allard has brought to life a legend that still circulates in France: the story of Philippa, who at the age of sixteen posed as a boy so that she could go to sea; and Aurelie, the woman she later came to love. They had no model of what it would be like for two women to love and live with one another, so they created their own form for that relationship.

LIFETIME GUARANTEE, by Alice Bloch, $7.00. In this personal journal of a woman faced with the impending death of her sister from cancer, Alice Bloch goes beyond her specific experiences to a moving exploration of the themes of survival, support, and affirmation of life.

A MISTRESS MODERATELY FAIR, by Katherine Sturtevant, $9.00. Shakespearean England provides the setting for this vivid story of two women — one a playwright, the other an actress — who fall in love. Margaret Featherstone and Amy Dudley romp through a London peopled by nameless thousands and the titled few in a historical romance that is the most entertaining and best researched you'll ever read.

THE WANDERGROUND, by Sally Miller Gearhart, $9.00. These absorbing, imaginative stories tell of a future women's culture, created in harmony with the natural world. The women depicted combine the control of mind and matter with a sensuous adherence to their own realities and history.

UNBROKEN TIES, by Carol S. Becker, $8.00. Through a series of nearly one hundred personal accounts and interviews, Dr. Carol Becker, a practicing psychotherapist, charts the various stages of lesbian breakups and examines the ways in which women maintain ties with their former lovers. Becker shows how the end of a relationship can be a time of personal growth and how former lovers can form the core of an alternative family network.

SUPPORT YOUR LOCAL BOOKSTORE

Most of the books described above are available at your nearest gay or feminist bookstore, and many of them will be available at other bookstores. If you can't get these books locally, order by mail using this form.

Enclosed is $_____ for the following books. (Add $1.00 postage when ordering just one book. If you order two or more, we'll pay the postage.)

1. _____

2. _____

3. _____

name: _____

address: _____

city: _____ state: _____ zip: _____

ALYSON PUBLICATIONS
Dept. H-58, 40 Plympton St., Boston, MA 02118

After December 31, 1992, please write for current catalog.